WORLD WIT
ENDLESS SHEEP

Alison Manning

APS BOOKS
Yorkshire

APS Books,
The Stables Field Lane,
Aberford,
West Yorkshire,
LS25 3AE

APS Books is a subsidiary of the APS Publications imprint

www.andrewsparke.com

First published worldwide by APS Books in 2022

A catalogue record for this book is available from the British Library

WORLD WITHOUT
ENDLESS SHEEP

Chapter One

TRAIN

JOSH peered through the dirty train window into the drizzle. He could just about make out the shape of a huge castle through the gloom. It looked like it might be worth exploring, but he was sure he would not get the chance. It was still about an hour to go to the end of his train ride and he had a bus to catch after that. He did not think there were any castles where he was going; he didn't think there would be anything interesting there at all. The castle disappeared into the growing darkness and Josh sighed and sank back down into his seat. He closed his eyes and tried not to think of the boredom ahead. He had no idea what was in store for him.

It just was not fair! His brother John was going to have lots of fun while he had to go to gloomy Wales for a dull three weeks without him. He tried not to blame his parents; he knew it was not their fault - they could not afford a proper holiday, but he thought they should try and understand him better. What was there in Wales, at least the obscure corner that he was going to? Nothing, as far as he could make out; no amusement arcades, no fun fair, no computer games - nothing to keep a boy of his age entertained. It would not have been so bad if John had come with him - they did not always get on but could have kept themselves entertained somehow. John, however, had gone to Spain with his friend Mikey, for three weeks on the sunny Costa Del Sol. Mikey was an only child and his parents had thoughtfully and generously agreed to pay for a friend of his to go on holiday with them to keep Mikey amused. They know more about their son's needs than my parents, thought Josh spitefully. Then he bit his lip as he immediately regretted the thought and tried to take it back. John had been the chosen one. John had been bragging about the trip for weeks which did not help. John was two years older than Josh and should have known better. Eventually John seemed to realise how much he was upsetting Josh and tried to gloat slightly less often. When Josh and his mum had gone to see him off at the airport he had softened slightly and the two boys shared an awkward embrace. John even said Josh could borrow his skateboard while he was away. Now that was something - John's skateboard was his pride and joy. Josh had been touched, but skateboarding was not really his thing and he had not bothered bringing it to Wales with him.

The trip to Wales was his parents' idea to try and make up for John's absence. It was the only thing they really had to offer. His dad was doing up an old cottage in Aberfawr, a small village in North West Wales. It belonged to a family friend who was paying well. Josh's dad had been unemployed for three months and was now trying to get back on his feet doing odd jobs for people. The work on the cottage would give him a steady income for a month at least and was too good to turn down. Josh's mum was a care assistant and had to stay at home and work. They both decided that a trip to the cottage to join his dad would do Josh good. His mum worried that Josh had been looking a bit pale and thought the sea air would put some colour in his cheeks. His dad thought that Josh would be better not moping around at home causing his mum stress, and that he would enjoy the beach and the walks around the village. Josh's dad had liked beaches and walks when he was young; he did not understand that kids today might like different things. If he was honest, he also thought Josh would be a bit of company for himself, and a useful assistant for some of the trickier jobs around the cottage. Josh thought he would rather have stayed at home, played on his mate's tablet, and lounging in front of the telly. There was no point arguing though; he knew his parents would not listen.

So here he was, stuck on this train on the way to the cottage which, as far as he could make out, was in a little village in the middle of nowhere. His dad was already there and was going to meet him from the train and take the last bus ride with him. Josh tried to look on the positive side, but had trouble thinking of one. There must be something to do in this place, what was it called? Abersomething? It could not be quite as dreary as the picture he had conjured up in his unhopeful mind, could it?

With a start Josh realised they were pulling into a station. He peered out into the gloom in haste and caught sight of a sign - it was his stop. He quickly grabbed his rucksack from the seat next to him, picked up his coat in his other hand, ran down the corridor to the train doors and leapt out of them, nearly colliding with a grumpy old woman who was just trying to get on. He muttered an embarrassed apology and hurried away to the station entrance where he was due to meet his dad.

The train was ten minutes late and his dad was standing in the doorway waiting, reading a free paper he'd picked up from the station. He looked up as Josh approached. "Hello son!" he said with a smile and put a hand out to ruffle Josh's hair. Josh tried not to flinch- he hated being treated like a small child. "Welcome to Wales!" his dad continued, "I hope you're going to like it in Aberfawr. There's a beach, though it's a bit pebbly, and lots of places to go for walks, when it's not raining too much of course."

Josh secretly wondered if it ever stopped raining in Wales, but tried his hardest to put on a cheerful front and show an interest. "Are there any rockpools?" he asked as they walked down the street towards the bus station. Josh personally was not that bothered about rockpools, but knew his dad was fascinated by them. Ever since they were tiny boys his dad had dragged them along beaches, using them as an excuse to poke around in slimy pools and lift up rocks looking for crabs and other creepy creatures. Josh had slipped on the seaweed at the side of one once and fallen in. He had rushed crying back to his mum. He couldn't see where the interest lay. He tried to pay attention as his dad weighed up the merits of Aberfawr beach.

"There are a few pools, not all that many though, but I saw a hermit crab in one the other day. They're not as good as the ones back in…" and he was off reminiscing about old holidays, with much fonder memories of rockpools than Josh.

They rounded a corner and reached the bus station. It was small by the standards Josh was used to. It was early evening now and still drizzling, so there were not many people around. Josh weighed up his surroundings as his dad was still talking about rockpools. His dad eventually realised Josh's attention was wandering and changed the subject. "I've bought some of your favourite cereal for you," he said, pulling a packet out of the carrier bag he held. He was starting to worry now that Josh would not like his stay at the cottage and was doing his best to be nice.

"Oh, thanks," said Josh quietly. He tried not to hold things against his dad, but was tired from his journey and didn't feel up to making much effort to talk. Fortunately, they didn't have to wait too long for the bus. His dad helped him on with his rucksack and he settled down, staring out of the window again. The relentless drizzle was still the same. He let out an involuntary sigh.

His dad placed a tentative arm around his shoulder, choosing to interpret the sigh as just a sign of tiredness. "Don't worry son, we'll be there soon."

It felt like a long time later, after much staring out at drizzly darkness and gloomy unidentifiable shapes, that his dad said: "Right Josh, here we are." His dad stood up, heaving the rucksack onto his shoulders and amassing the shopping bags that had lain at his feet.

Josh dragged himself to his feet and drew his coat tight around him, bracing himself for the cold and wet that hit him as soon as he stepped off the bus. He was really tired now and had barely enough energy to glance around him, his exhaustion having drained his curiosity. He could make out a handful of terraced houses, a pub and a large looming thing that was probably a church tower. His dad led him over the road from the bus stop to a house in the middle of the terrace and fished in his pocket for his keys.

"Here we are Josh," he said, "Home at last- for the next few weeks at least. Hopefully the weather will brighten up for us soon."

Chapter Two:

RAIN

BUT the next morning it was still raining.

Josh explored the little house which didn't take long. His dad had given him the larger bedroom at the front, so if he opened the window and craned his neck out, he could just about see the sea - about half a mile away he guessed. It looked grey and uninviting and his head was being splashed with rain, so he pulled it in again quickly and went to look round the rest of the house. His dad had the room in the middle, bare except for a blow-up mattress on the floor. The only other room upstairs was the bathroom - serviceable but old and shabby-looking with grimy walls. Josh noted the boxes of tiles in the corner and remembered this was one of the jobs his dad had been employed to do. Downstairs was equally dull. There was a longish thin lounge with a table at one end which served as a dining area. The only other room downstairs was the kitchen which, like the bathroom, showed signs of age. It was cold and damp with patches of discoloured plaster.

His dad came in and caught him looking at one of the worst patches. "Nothing a good scrub and a lick of paint won't cure" he exclaimed in an attempt to maintain his cheery demeanour of the night before. "In fact, it's next on the list. You can give me a hand if you like, till this rain clears up. I'm afraid it's a bit too wet out there to have much fun yet", he added with a jerk of his head towards the window.

Josh didn't think there was much chance of fun inside or out, whatever the weather, but kept his thoughts to himself. It was his first day; things might yet brighten up; he could at least hope. It did look particularly dark outside the window but as Josh went for a closer look he noticed this was partly because the cottage was set in the side of a hill and the back of it faced out to rocks and steep steps which presumably led up to the rest of the garden. Oddly enough he didn't feel tempted to explore outside with the constant rain lashing down at the windows - the drips he had had from sticking his head out of the bedroom window were enough for now.

He noticed that his dad, whistling to himself, had got bacon out of the fridge and was in the process of putting it under the little grill. Bacon butties for breakfast was a bonus at least! His health and price conscious mum rarely allowed that at home.

A full tummy kept him relatively upbeat for most of that day, in the circumstances. He was surprised to find a strange satisfaction in scrubbing the grime off the kitchen walls to reveal the white paint beneath. When the new white paint went on it was even better, seeing a new bright sparkly clean kitchen emerge. His dad was a bit cautious about letting him loose with the paint, but Josh was particularly careful as he had promised to be, and his dad visibly relaxed as he saw the care Josh took over the painting and even exclaimed "You're good at this son, you could come into business with me when you're older!" Josh just smiled a little in response. Painting was ok for a bit, slightly more enjoyable than he had thought it might be, but he couldn't see himself doing this for a career.

As the second day dawned, he did not even need to open the curtains to reveal what the constant pitter patter had already told his ears; it was still raining, and hard. He carried on helping his dad, but the going was harder today. The novelty was starting to wear off. And there were no bacon sandwiches to sustain him. Josh wasn't sure if this was just because they'd eaten all the bacon the day before and it was too wet to go to the shops, or if the first day's breakfast feast had been a one-off welcoming meal. He didn't have the heart to ask.

The rain was so constant that he still had not ventured beyond the walls of the cottage, but he promised himself that if the weather was not any better the next day he would try and persuade his dad to let him go out anyway. He was starting to feel cooped up and enclosed. The paint fumes were not really helping either, despite the constantly propped open window that seemed much more keen on letting in a chilly draft than letting out the nauseous smell of decorating.

The next day when he awoke, he lay in bed and listened before he even opened his eyes. The loud pitter-pattering of the last two days seemed to have eased off. He cautiously opened the curtains to reveal that the constant torrent had slowed to a constant drizzle. He sighed resignedly to himself and thought, *Oh well, at least it's a step in the right direction. I might at least make it outside as far as the shop…*

He made his proposal to his dad at breakfast (cornflakes, disappointingly). "I was thinking dad, as the rain's easing off, that I might pop out later and get us some things from the shops. Is there anything you'd like? Bacon maybe?"

His dad laughed briefly, "Yes, we can get some more bacon if you like. I know you love your breakfast treat, but I'd like a hand finishing off these skirting boards first. Then I'll come with you later on and show you where the shop is."

Although Josh had yet to walk anywhere in the village other than from the bus stop to the cottage (about ten metres!) he had the distinct impression that it was not really big enough to get very lost in. Still, he thought charitably, *Dad probably wants a break from the paint fumes too.* So he agreed quietly and got on with the job in hand.

After a quick sandwich break for lunch (which they ate upstairs in Josh's room, in a partly futile attempt to escape the fumes, they donned waterproofs and ventured outside. Josh took a deep breath of the drizzly air. Damp was his first impression, but with the analytical skills of a wine taster he sniffed on and decided it was also fresh and breezy, with a tantalising hint of salt, and blissfully paint free!

The large grey looming thing he had glimpsed when he first arrived did indeed prove to be an old church with an impressively solid-looking tower, surrounded on all sides by a sprawling graveyard. A stony, partly-overgrown path led down the side of the graveyard.

"That Josh", said his dad in a cheery voice, "leads to the beach. Though I'm afraid it's a bit too wet and slippy to attempt today after all these downpours we've been having."

Josh felt no more than mild disappointment. The path did not look too inviting, but he did think it would be nice to breathe soon further away from the paint-fume-filled cottage.

The shop proved to be the local petrol station, but still had a reasonable range of stuff. Clearly, as it seemed to be the only shop in the village, it played a valuable role in serving the local community, as well as the occasional holiday-maker. Josh not only managed to persuade his dad to buy bacon, but also sausages, eggs and a small tub of ice cream. "We can pretend it's sunny, even if it's not" said his dad.

Josh was grateful but his thoughts kept straying to John in Spain, doubtless enjoying endless sunshine.

His dad seemed to read his mind, "At least we're not in danger of getting sunburnt like John."

Josh though this a scant consolation.

He didn't see much of note on his way back to the cottage - just a scattering of houses of varying degrees of oldness spreading out to the edges of the village, which seemed a bit larger than he'd first thought. He also caught tantalising glimpses of the mountains behind the village emerging from the mist that must have shrouded them for the last few days. *This place might actually look quite scenic when the sun comes out, if it ever does,* he found himself thinking charitably, perhaps cheered by the prospect of ice cream and bacon the next day.

Chapter Three

DOMAIN

THE next day indeed was bright and full of promise. Josh awoke to a stray ray of light beaming through the gap in the curtains which he had carelessly drawn the night before. He threw them back and looked out. The sky was blue, if not entirely cloudless, and he risked sticking his head out again to breath in deeply of the fresh, rain-free air.

He didn't even linger to savour his breakfast bacon butty after his dad suggested they might both take the morning off for a stroll to the local beach in honour of the newly discovered sunshine.

Despite his initial reservations about the area, after being cooped up for three days Josh found he was desperate to go further than the shop and he was eager to explore what the local beach had to offer. So, he soon found himself hurrying down the overgrown path by the side of the church with his dad, who either didn't seem to think Josh was capable of finding anywhere by himself, or welcomed the excuse for a morning off as much as Josh did. The path ran alongside a few well-spaced houses, then under some trees to a kissing gate, which led in turn through to a track with tarmac at the sides but a grass strip down the middle, looking, despite which, as though the occasional vehicle ventured down it.

A low mooing alerted him to the fact that there were cows in the field to the side. There also seemed to be a lot of sheep. It was a pleasant amble downhill.

His dad was in good spirits "You can almost smell the salt in the air can't you!" he smiled.

Josh sniffed obediently "Almost," he agreed.

The track turned a corner and there was another gate going off to the side. Josh's dad reached it first, drew back the bolt and held it open for Josh to go through.

This section of the path was a narrow cutting between bushes on either side. "Looks like there'll be blackberries here come September," commented Josh's dad, examining the nondescript brambles which Josh was ignoring and heading off along the path, impatiently thinking they must be near the sea now. He did start to think he could smell salt now, so he knew they must be close.

The path came to an abrupt halt at the top of some steep steps downwards, and there beyond them was a beach, a bit of sand with larger rocks closest to them, followed by a more rocky/ pooly/ seaweedy section, and beyond that the sea itself, a giant grey-blue expanse topped with frothy white waves extending out into the distance. It was a sight guaranteed to bring a smile to anyone like Josh who lived in a land-locked city far from the coast and rarely made it to the sea. Ok, so it wasn't Spain, but the sky was mostly blue, the now-definitely salt air was brisk and fresh and the waves, though not quite inviting, were somehow kind of enticing.

"Come on son, what are you waiting for?"

Josh's dad had come up behind him patting him on the back. Without realising it, Josh had stopped in his tracks, taken aback by the expansive view before him. With the pressure of his dad's hand on his back he hurried ahead down the steps, taking care nevertheless to hold onto the rickety old metal handrail next to them as the steps themselves were uneven and slippery. Soon he was down them on the beach itself, taking in every detail such as the stream to his left, scuttling over the stones into the sea.

"Is it ok if I take my trainers and socks off, Dad?" Josh asked, sitting on a rock and starting to unfasten his laces before waiting for an answer.

"Of course," grinned his dad, delighting in Josh's obvious pleasure in the simple delights of the beach that in another time or other company he might have tried to hide.

Soon Josh had tucked his socks inside his trainers, rolled his trousers up and was splashing in the little stream, edging further out onto the beach. He quickly discovered that many of the rocks were rather hard under foot, and the smoother ones slightly further down were so seaweed-coated that they were almost too slippery to even attempt to stand on without risking a fall into a rockpool. He didn't want to repeat the rockpool incident from when he was tiny, so he opted for walking along the sandy patches of the beach. These were still pebble-strewn but the stones were smaller and less harsh on his feet, and contained fragments of shells that glinted in the light and mildly intrigued him.

"Let's walk this way a bit," said his dad, leading the way along the mainly sandy stretch, sensing Josh's hesitation about the more rocky sections. Josh looked up along the beach, having been carefully watching where he placed each foot, and noticed that the sea was not an endless expanse as it had first seemed from the view at the top of the steps because a sizeable island was rising out of it not too far in the distance.

His dad again followed his gaze, "That's Anglesey out there, that is", he said, always happy to commentate, "It doesn't look too far as the crow flies, or the gull swims," chuckling at his own witticism, "But to get to it the best way is to go all the way along the road nearly to Bangor and cross the bridge."

"There's a bridge to it?" asked Josh, interested in spite of himself, then remembered that they had no car here and, if it was a long journey by road, it was almost certainly too long or too difficult by bus, so as his dad nodded assent he glanced around for a way to change the subject.

It was then that he noticed a swing sticking up from above the small cliff at the top of the beach. It was more like a fun tyre swing you could climb on than a little kids' one. It seemed a bit odd being so far from the road; he'd seen nothing but grazing fields and trees as they neared the beach.

"Hey what's that over there?" he called to his dad, heading up the beach. This wasn't really a good plan to enable him to see more as the swing just promptly disappeared from sight behind the top of the cliff, but it did have the desired effect of distracting his dad. As they walked further along the beach there was a dip between the cliffs with a steep grassy slope leading up towards where he had sighted the swing, and just up from it he noticed something else that looked out of place - a couple of picnic benches. They weren't at all the kind of facilities he'd expect on this wild, rocky, windswept and, seemingly, mostly-deserted beach (they'd seen a dog walker or two at most, in all their time on the beach, as far as they could see along the stretch they were on till it rounded a corner).

Nevertheless, Josh was about to suggest they come down here and have a picnic one day (how much nicer that would be than eating in the paint-fume-filled cottage!) when his dad spoke first. "Sorry Josh, they're not for us to use - look at the sign," and he pointed at a wooden board set in the side of the bottom of the cliff that Josh had somehow missed. It was hand-painted in a murky brown colour, so not the most eye-catching, but it clearly proclaimed "KEEP OUT! PRIVATE!" in rounded capitals. As a warning it was intriguing in itself, and just seemed to make the picnic benches and swing even more mysterious. *Why are they there*, Josh wondered to himself, *so far from any noticeable building, and why this slightly obscured warning sign? Who do the benches belong to and why are they so keen to keep other people away from them?*

He couldn't stand there pondering for long however, as his dad suddenly raced off down the beach proclaiming "Can't catch me!" in a challenge Josh was unable to turn down, racing away after him back in the direction of to the cottage so his dad could do more work in the afternoon.

That night Josh deliberately left a gap between his thin curtains, in the hope of being awoken by another sunbeam heralding another sunny day.

Chapter Four

ENTERTAIN

AND the next day he was not disappointed!

He awoke to a new beam of light, pulled back his curtains and then ambled downstairs to breakfast.

His dad seemed in a cheery mood. "Blimey Josh, sunshine two days in a row; either you've brought me luck or it must be a miracle!."

Josh thought he had conveniently forgotten about the three solid days of rain that had followed his arrival, but thought he'd try and capitalise on his dad's good mood. "Can we go to the beach again today dad, please?."

His dad looked thoughtful. "I've got a few bits of painting I need to finish off this morning, but we can't have you missing out on the sunshine, and I can't really do the next bit till they're dry anyway. So this afternoon I'll take you on a trip up to a little town up the coast I've heard about. It's supposed to have a much better beach than the local one here, a lot more sand, and I'll treat you to fish and chips on the way back.

In some ways Josh was disappointed not to be going back to the local beach. He'd been looking forward to exploring a bit more, and he really wanted to find out about the strange forbidden picnic benches. On the other hand…fish and chips were his favourite, and in his opinion you couldn't beat them eaten out of the packet by the seaside bathed in vinegar. "You're on!" he said.

He spent the morning alternately helping and keeping out of the way and checking the bus timetable his dad had entrusted to him with their destination circled. "The bus doesn't quite go right to the coast," said dad, "So we might have to walk for a bit at the other end, but it's not too far and should be a pleasant walk."

As soon as his dad had finished, changed out of his painting clothes and scrubbed himself clean, they wolfed down some sandwiches and cups of tea and hurried out to the bus stop, just over the road from the house. They didn't have to wait long for a bus and they travelled on it for about fifteen minutes, on a long straight road parallel to the coast. Josh gazed out at the sea and listened to the lilt of Welsh voices around him, a bit different from where he came from. He supposed this must have been the route the bus had taken from the train station the other day, but it had been too dark to tell and he had been too tired from the journey to be bothered. He thought back to how he had felt on that journey, not really filled with hope for the prospect ahead, but it wasn't really turning out to be as bad as he'd feared. When the sun came out it was quite a pleasant area to be in.

He turned his head from the sea and glanced out of the other side of the bus at the mountains rising majestically. Maybe he'd even suggest to his dad climbing one at one point. He wasn't quite sure what had come over him; he wasn't usually this full of love for the great outdoors. Maybe he wouldn't suggest a mountain climb just yet.

"This one's ours" said his dad, rising and pressing the bell on the pole next to him, swinging his small rucksack onto his shoulder and beckoning for Josh to follow him.

It proved a longer walk than Josh had expected to the beach, not helped by taking a wrong turning down a country lane that ended in a dead end, so he was a bit fed up, but pleased when they finally rounded a corner to see a car park, backed by the promenade, a high sea wall, and then the beach. It was certainly much sandier than their local beach, and split in two by an interesting small hillock that seemed to just rise up in the middle of the beach, as if a giant sandcastle had been left behind, failed to get washed away, and sprouted grass. Josh eyed it with curiosity.

"We can have a stroll up there later if you like" said his dad, "But first I'm afraid I'm desperate for a cup of tea."

Not really disappointed to have the climb delayed after the long walk from the bus stop, Josh tagged after his dad towards the row of shops opposite the beach car park. His dad seemed to be heading for a small café in the middle, that seemed quite basic but had a few seats outside facing the beach. "Did you want a drink, Josh?" he asked, but Josh had spotted something else. On the far side of the café there was a tiny amusement arcade with a handful of machines including Josh's favourite coin pusher machine, where you put two-penny pieces into a slot, carefully calculated to fall in a certain place so when the shelves moved in and out more coins were knocked onto the lower shelf and then, in turn, off that and into the slot below ready to be retrieved by Josh's eager hand. His dad followed his gaze, "Alright son, off you go and try your luck for ten minutes while I drink my tea, then we'll go on the beach." He put his hand in his trouser pocket and picked out a handful of coins. "Here you go" he added, selecting the 2ps and holding them out to Josh grinning, "I know which your favourite is."

So Josh took the proffered coins and wandered over to the amusement arcade. He took in the other machines at a quick glance, and then made a beeline for his favourite coin pusher machine. He spent a long time weighing up his strategy, carefully working out which slot and at what time to push the coin in before committing each one into the machine. At first, he had no luck, but proceeded slowly, weighing up each attempt, and had just heard the resounding, gratifying clunk of coins into the dispenser when his dad came up behind him and he realised he had lost all track of time. "Ready for the beach now?" his dad asked. "Yes, now I am!" replied Josh grinning, scooping the coins out of the machine into a pile in his hand. He offered some back to his dad who shook his head "No, you keep them, Josh, they're your winnings." So Josh added them to his wallet and replaced it in his pocket with its newly-formed bulge, and they headed over the road to the beach.

Josh's dad produced a small picnic blanket from his rucksack, spread it out on a sandy spot, and proceeded to sit on it and start unlacing his shoes. "Race you to the sea!" he proclaimed. Josh sat down next to him and started pulling his trainers off, the tide seemed to be a long way out. He threw his socks inside his trainers and started jogging towards the thin line of water in the distance. His dad weighed the blanket down with the rucksack and followed.

As his first toes hit the water Josh gave an involuntary shriek- the water was freezing! "Well, this is Wales you know!" laughed his dad, coming up behind and dipping his toes in the water without so much as a squeal. After a couple of minutes of dodging waves and hopping from foot to foot, Josh's toes acclimatised and it didn't feel so bad. His dad had returned to the rucksack and came back brandishing two old but sturdy looking plastic spades and a small round bucket. "I found these under the stairs in the cottage, thought they might come in useful." Josh would ordinarily have thought himself too old for building sandcastles, but the blank canvas of the beach looked inviting and there was no one there to see him and ruin his street cred. "Alright then" he declared, snatching one of the spades from his father's outstretched hand, "But we're building a proper fortress, not a silly little kids' sandcastle"

"Ok, you're on," was the reply, and they worked together to construct battlements, mounds and tunnels, with a long channel for the returning tide to follow along, waterfalling down into the moat they had created together. Gradually, the incoming water got more and more powerful, starting to wash away first the moat, then the outlying towers, and then the main mound of fortress itself. Josh and his dad were ankle deep in water at this point "Quick, catch the spades before they float away," yelled his dad, adding "I'll grab the bucket," and together they grabbed their implements and ran back laughing to the picnic blanket. "Fish and chip time now?" said his dad enquiringly.

"Yes please!" said Josh. He had enjoyed his time on the beach, far more than his limited expectations, but suddenly realised he was exceedingly hungry. They pulled on socks and shoes and headed back up the beach to a chip shop Josh hadn't previously noticed at the side of the car park. "Usual?" asked his dad.

"Yes please" affirmed Josh, and in no time at all they were sitting on a bench on the promenade wall, looking out to sea and tucking into their delicious feast. "Right," said his dad, looking at his watch, as they each scraped the last scrap out of their polystyrene containers, "I think we've got just enough time for a quick run up that hill before we need to head back to the bus stop." "You must be joking", mock-grimaced Josh, but stood up nevertheless and hastily stashed his empty container in the nearby bin, ready for a quick start if his dad proved not to be joking.

Apparently he wasn't, "Off we go then!" he said, stowing his own container in the bin and marching off grinning just ahead of Josh. It wasn't really a run, more of a quick walk, and actually proved to be quite enjoyable. It wasn't too far to the top, they were there in less than 10 minutes and could admire the impressive view of both sides of the beach, and the coastline stretching away into the distance. Josh noticed that you could see more of Anglesey from here too, rising majestically out of the sea, but chose not to mention it. His dad looked at his watch again "Gosh, the bus goes in 20 minutes, better race down the other side." So they ran down together, finding it strangely exhilarating with the fresh sea air and strong breeze, though it was slightly grating on their knees, and continued at a steady jog all the way back to the bus stop. It did not seem as far to Josh as before, now they knew where they were going, and they managed to arrive in time with a couple of minutes to spare.

Chapter Five

ANCIENT NAME

THE next day was Saturday, but his dad said he still needed to crack on with the tiling having taken the previous afternoon off. Although it was not as bright as the previous day - in fact it was distinctly cloudy - Josh still thought it would be a shame to waste a day when it was not actually raining, so he decided to ask his dad if he could go out by himself.

His dad gave it some thought, "OK" he said at last, "I can't see the harm in it, but I don't want you wandering too far from the cottage. You don't know your way round properly yet, and watch the main road. Maybe you could just go for a wander around the churchyard opposite, I'm sure no one will mind. It will get you a bit of fresh air, and there's some interesting birds flying around there. Perhaps you could get a closer look."

Josh inwardly sighed. Again this was one of his dad's interests that he tried to ignite in Josh. Josh could kindle a passing interest at times, but nothing like his dad's passion but at least he had been granted freedom for a while, if only within a hundred metres of the cottage! So he stuck an apple in his hoodie pocket in case he got hungry, and let himself out of the door quickly before his dad could change his mind.

He crossed the road carefully, thinking to himself that he had more sense than some people gave him credit for.

The entrance to the churchyard was through a kind of arched gateway which looked very old in itself, with its heavy stone and slightly odd angles. The church itself looked even older, though possibly he thought it might be a mixture of ages, as it looked a bit of an uneven shape with extra bits sticking out at the side, and he remembered learning about old buildings being added to and adapted over time in history at school. He thought he'd leave examining the church any more till later, and start with a mooch around the gravestones. These were a fascinating mixture of very old ones with worn inscriptions that were hard to read, slightly more modern ones with intriguing Welsh names, and assorted lopsided ones in between. He quickly began to notice that certain surnames featured a lot; Williams, for instance, and wasn't sure if this was because lots of extended families had lived in the village, or if they were just common Welsh names, or both. Although not huge, the churchyard was big enough to contain a lot of graves. Josh suspected no more would fit in now.

He eventually worked his way round to the far side of the church building and noticed there was a gate leading through to the path they had taken down to the local beach. He tried the handle but it appeared to be padlocked. A little further round he spotted a tall stone with a hole in the middle near the top that looked interesting. On closer inspection it looked to be some kind of sundial, with markings round the side. Again, it looked very old, and the figures on it were very faint, making it hard to try and decipher a reading from it.

Josh moved on to the very far corner of the graveyard from the gate he had come in at. This seemed to be a very old, if neglected part of the graveyard. The graves that were there were mostly flat on the ground, though Josh wasn't sure if that is where they had started off or if they had just fallen over the centuries. It was more overgrown here and there were a few trees and a tangle of bushes by the stone wall marking the perimeter.

Suddenly, from quite low down in the shrubbery, a flash of red flew out and stopped upon the wall nearby. It was a robin, who stopped and cocked his head at Josh, weighing him up to see if he was friend or foe. Clearly he decided he wasn't of any interest at all as he quickly flew off into the nearby field. Josh felt partly amused and mildly put out at being so easily dismissed by the bird. But it seemed only a few seconds before the robin was back, cocking his head at Josh again on top of the wall, this time with a small wriggly green thing in its beak. He then disappeared off into the bushes again at the exact point it had emerged earlier. It must have a nest!

Suddenly, but faintly, Josh heard shrill, quick cheeps, as the robin's chicks clearly vied for consumption of the caterpillar. It went quiet again as the robin remerged and disappeared back into the field. Suddenly, in a ruffle of feathers, it reappeared again on the wall, but then Josh realised this was a browner version, the female, still with a cheeky cock of its head, clutching a worm this time. It darted back into the nest followed by the red-breasted male with another worm, eyeing up Josh from the wall with its beady eye while it waited for its mate to leave the nest so he could go in and take his turn feeding the hidden cheeping chicks. *They certainly keep you two busy!* thought Josh to himself.

Something wet landed on his shoulder. He momentarily worried it was a present from one of the birds flying overhead, but when there was another drop on his other shoulder, and more on his head, he realised it was starting to rain, huge droplets, heavy and fast. Unwilling to rush back to the cottage for shelter, and thinking he would get soaked on the way, he hurried round the church building, thinking in its higgledy-piggledy layout it must have some kind of overhang that would afford him shelter. To his delight he found a roomy covered porchway, walls on both sides and a huge wooden door on the third. He tried the heavy door handle, just in case, but it was locked as he had thought it would be. Still, it was no matter; though he was curious to see the inside, there was plenty of space for him to shelter from the now torrential rain.

He remembered the apple in his pocket, took it out, gave it a quick wipe and started munching on it as he occupied himself by reading the notices stuck on the walls. One of them concerned service times, and he noticed there was a service the next day which declared it was jointly in English and Welsh. He remembered being fascinated by the lyrical Welsh voices on the bus. He wasn't usually much of a church goer - Christmas and Easter and maybe Mothers' Day when mum dragged him along were about his limits - but a bilingual service somehow sounded quite intriguing. Especially, as he thought to himself, *It would give me a chance to see the inside of this beguiling building.* He could not work out how the floor plan would work inside from the odd layout of the outside. There seemed to be almost two separate buildings connected by a long thin part. He checked the time again – eleven a.m. He thought that would give him enough time for a Sunday lie-in, and his dad had said he would not be working on the Sunday. He also noted that the same vicar who was down to lead the service was down to lead another one elsewhere at twelve-thirty, so he was sure it would not be too long. Peering out again into the graveyard from his dry refuge, he resolved to ask his dad if they could come to the service the next day. He also noticed that the rain was slowing down now, and realised that his dad might be worried about him if he had noticed the downpour and the fact that Josh had not taken his coat. So, apple core in hand, he headed back to the cottage with the dual purpose in mind of reassuring his dad and asking about the next morning, with an extra wonder if it was nearly lunchtime yet...

Chapter Six

REFRAIN

HIS dad, though mildly surprised, had agreed readily enough to Josh's request to go to the church service. He too had a curiosity about this imposing ancient building so close to their temporary home. The bells summoned them the next morning, ringing out from the tall battlemented tower, as they crossed the road to the church. This time the large wooden door was wide open, and they entered, slightly nervously, to be warmly greeted by a lady on the door who was handing out service books and hymn sheets. "Sit wherever you like," she said, ushering them forward into the lofty interior.

It seemed even taller on the inside, if that was possible, but wasn't as gloomy as Josh had thought it might be. He had somehow expected a slightly spooky dark interior, but the large arched windows set high in the whitewashed walls let in lots of light. There were chairs laid out on two sides of the main bit of the interior, with an aisle down the middle, leading towards what seemed to be the front of the church, initially with a wider section, with bits jutting out on either side, resembling the shape of a cross, then tapering out in the very front part, which was sectioned off by an elaborate wooden screen but had a large open doorway through, showing what looked like a few choir stalls and an altar, covered with a cloth.

They edged forwards and picked seats on the right-hand side, Josh making sure he was at the end nearest the wall, so he could observe everything from a safe distance. Once seated, he turned around and glanced behind him. He could just about make out a corridor going off to the side, which must lead to another part of the sprawling building. Whilst waiting for it to start, he looked at the books they had been handed on the way in. He noticed with interest that one page had the order of service in English while the opposite was in

Welsh. He studied the two side by side wondering if he could work out what some of the Welsh words meant. It looked a hard language to master. He turned to the wall next to him, intrigued by a zig zag metal structure mounted on it. He could not imagine what it might be for. It had widespread handles at one end and what looked like spiky salad servers at the other. He noticed there was a small label underneath and peered closer. The sign read *Dog tongs (1815) used to expel rowdy dogs from the church.* The vision of barking dogs running uncontrollably round the quiet church was so funny that Josh had to suppress a giggle and put a hand over his mouth to hide his grin as he hastily turned back to the front as the service began.

There were only a handful of others in the church, most much older than his dad, yet alone Josh. He wasn't quite sure what he'd let himself in for. Despite that, he enjoyed the opening hymn. He had been in the school choir when he was younger and secretly enjoyed a good burst of song. He was intrigued when the singing changed to Welsh in the third verse, though it defeated his efforts to join in. As the service went on he tried to focus, following the words in the service book, but his mind started to wander as boredom crept in. Odd words from the liturgy crept through into his daydreaming, however…. "World Without End" the vicar intoned and Josh was thinking *Yes, that's what I thought Wales would be like… a world without end…going on and on…. Never-ending drizzle, lots of sheep and nothing to do. And ok, there is not a lot to do, but it's not too bad when the rain stops. Ok it's still dull at times, but the beach isn't too bad….*

Josh was roused from his reverie by the closing hymn, a stirring rendition of *And Can it Be*, with the men echoing the women at the end of each verse. There were not many people there, but they were all joining in with gusto, backing up Josh's other stereotypical view of the Welsh that they were good at singing. It certainly woke Josh up.

Afterwards the vicar said the final blessing and moved towards the door of the church, where he stood and shook hands with everyone on their way out. He gave a cheery greeting and a firm handshake to Josh's dad: "Welcome, I haven't seen you before, have I? Are you here on holiday? Staying in the Village?"

Josh's dad launched into a brief explanation of what had brought them there while Josh deposited his hymn sheet and service book on the growing pile on the table nearby. He noticed there were some leaflets about the history of the church. Josh's dad had finished his explanation now and the vicar turned to see what Josh was looking at. "Ah, you're interested in the history of our church. Do help yourself to a leaflet. It has a long and fascinating history. You know, of course, it was an important point for pilgrims on their way to Bardsey Island? Josh hadn't known and had no idea where Bardsey Island was, but managed to make some noise of agreement and picked up a leaflet. Starting to look through it, he noticed there was a black and white illustration of the dog tongs that had entertained him earlier, as well as drawings of other artefacts around the church, such as an old wooden chest. Suddenly one bit jumped out at him, entitled *Monks' passageway*. He read on with interest.

Apparently when monks had lived there many centuries earlier, they had farmed the land between the church and the sea. It was believed they had had a hidden underground passageway between the two in case it was ever needed. Josh wasn't quite sure what emergency might mean the monks needed a tunnel, but his history was a bit hazy. He read on to find out more, but it ended disappointingly with *No one now knows if or where it existed*.

He glanced up as the vicar said, "Sorry I really do have to go now" and headed out of the door, to which his dad inexplicably responded "Bye, thank you, see you tomorrow."

Josh's puzzled stare told his dad that he had missed a significant part of the conversation. "Oh, come on Josh," he said teasingly, "Were you not listening at all?"

"Actually, the leaflet was quite interesting," replied Josh, holding it up somewhat sheepishly. "What did I miss?"

"He was telling us about the history of the church, about the original chapel down that passageway." He nodded disappointingly not underground but down the corridor Josh had noted earlier. "And about how they added this bit of the church later. But then he apologised and said he had to go as he had another service to lead, but he invited us round to his house for tea tomorrow so he can tell us more. He seems to love sharing the history of this place, and I must admit it's rather fascinating, and it seemed rude not to accept."

"Ok," said Josh, his mind whirring and catching up slowly, part of it still dwelling in the elusive underground passageway, "Where does he live?"

"At the vicarage, just up the road, don't worry I know the one. Six p.m. tomorrow"

"Ok," repeated Josh.

"Now listen", said his dad conspiratorially, "How about a treat as it's Sunday? Let's go have a roast dinner at that pub up the road."

Josh's dad wasn't the greatest cook and anyway it was difficult to do much beyond bacon sandwiches in the small, not yet properly equipped, paint-fumed kitchen, so Josh readily agreed. His dad knew the way to his heart.

Ten minutes later saw them seated in a snug by the window in the pub up the road.

Josh pulled the leaflet out of his pocket and studied it as his dad went to order their food at the bar - roast beef and Yorkshire pudding for them both. It sounded tasty, if not very Welsh! Josh had noticed on the back page of the leaflet there was a roughly drawn map, showing the church, the centre of the village to the south of it, and to the north the sea. A slightly wiggly line indicated the path to the beach he had walked down with his dad. He tried to puzzle out where the passageway might be. The only land directly between the church and the sea, other than fields of endless sheep, a handful of cows, and a couple of horses, must be the strange bit he had glimpsed with the picnic benches and swings. He noticed a couple of angular shapes in the middle, set slightly back from the coast. There must be a be a building there after all he thought, somehow hidden behind the cliffs. Try as he might, he couldn't work out where the tunnel might be though.

Later that afternoon, after they had feasted on their delicious roast dinner, and left a suitable interval for their food to go down, they headed back down the path to the beach again. The sky was a bit grey but the rain was holding off. The tide was slowly going out and Josh's dad had a great time carefully edging round the rock pools and seeing what the receding waves had left behind. He called Josh excitedly with each new find, his favourite being a tiny hermit crab which peeped out of its shell and then scuttled away nervously and tried to hide itself in the sand at the bottom of the rock pool. Josh did not object and tried to show an interest in the things his dad was pointing out to him, but his real fascination lay with the half-glimpsed picnic benches, trying to peer up over the clifftop for a sight of the hidden buildings, and trying to puzzle out where the mysterious tunnel might have come out, if it had ever existed.

Chapter Seven

OWAIN

NEXT morning the grey skies had opened and the rain was pouring down.

"Never mind," said Josh's dad, "It will give me a chance to get on with some work without getting distracted. You couldn't give me a hand with these bathroom titles could you please, Josh?"

So Josh dutifully stayed in and helped his dad, which at first seemed to mainly consist of passing things and holding them in place, while his dad did the trickier jobs such as cutting the tiles to shape. As the day progressed, however, Josh's dad gradually gave him more and more responsibility and even let him do some of the grouting between the tiles. He was amazed when his dad glanced at his watch and declared that it was five o'clock and they should pack up for the day and get ready for tea with the vicar at six. Josh had thought he might want to laze around more but the work had kept him busy, helping the day pass quickly and had given him a great sense of achievement when he stood back at the end of the day and saw how much they had done. They each scrubbed the day's grime and grout off their hands and got changed into fresh clothes. They were just putting their shoes on and heading out of the door when his dad exclaimed suddenly "Hey, do you think we should take something with us? Is that the done thing?"

Josh just stared at him cluelessly but that was fine as his dad was mostly asking himself anyway. "I know what," he concluded eventually, "Let's pop by the shop on the way and see if inspiration strikes us."

So they headed out to the shop in search of ideas. His dad paused in the alcohol section. "Do you think they drink wine? Probably, but not certainly, and we don't know what sort...."

"How about chocolates?" said Josh, who was round the corner, drawn imperceptibly to the confectionary section. "Everybody likes chocolates."

"You know, Josh, I think you're right" said his dad, quickly grabbing a box and taking it to the checkout. As they went out of the shop and back past the cottage, he hastily peeled off the price label and stowed the chocolates under his arm. "The vicarage should be just down here Josh, a bit past the church on the edge of the village" he said, strolling off.

They arrived exactly on time to a clearly labelled, solid-looking stone house and his dad rang the bell. The vicar answered, all jovial, and full of gratitude as he accepted the proffered chocolates. "Thank you, that's very kind of you, but you shouldn't have."

"Our pleasure, Reverend," said Josh's dad slightly hesitantly, uncertain about the etiquette of addressing vicars, "It was very kind of you to have us round."

"Call me Owain," said the vicar, taking their coats to hang on the banister and ushering them through to a cosy kitchen diner where an equally cheerful-looking woman was putting glasses on the table. "And this is my wife Kathryn."

"Pleased to meet you," said Josh's dad, shaking hands, "I'm Darren and this is my son Josh."

"Hi," said Josh, a sudden shyness overtaking him. He had not realised that the vicar was married but, to be fair, he had not really been paying attention to the conversation with him the previous day.

"Take a seat, take a seat" said Owain the vicar, "Don't stand on ceremony, I expect you're hungry. Food will be ready soon."

"It's shepherd's pie," said Kathryn, "I hope you like it."

"My favourite," said Darren, "And Josh eats practically anything, he's a growing boy."

"Except olives," said Josh, a bit put out by his dad's patronising tone.

"Ah, don't worry," said Kathryn, "There aren't any olives in our shepherd's pie - you're safe."

The table was already laid with a red cloth and plates and cutlery. It was a cosy room with bookcases and a French window at one end by the dining table they were at, and a huge range cooker at the other end. It was nice to be in the warm and dry with the prospect of a hot decent meal after getting damp in the rain on the way there.

A timer buzzed. "Ah, that should be ready now" said Kathryn, "Would you check please, dear?"

Owain opened the oven and peered inside. "Looks good to me!" he said, pulling out a large rectangular dish with both hands in thickly-wadded oven gloves and setting it upon a dragon trivet in the middle of the table. Kathyrn took the oven gloves from him and went back to the oven, switching it off and returning with a garlic baguette.

"I thought we'd do some garlic bread as well" she said, "Just in case you didn't like shepherd's pie and were too polite to say. Or were just extra hungry."

Josh started to warm to these people who gave options and planned ahead of possible scenarios to ensure they could keep their guests happy. He made an effort to be sociable, "Sounds lovely, thanks."

After all the food was set before them, Josh was about to tuck in eagerly when Owain said "Let's say Grace," and Josh hastily replaced his knife and fork on the table. When the vicar had prayed and given thanks for the food, Josh picked them up carefully again and started tucking in - it was delicious.

"So Darren," said Kathryn, "Owain tells me you're helping to do up a house in the village. How's it going?"

Josh absorbed himself in his food as his dad launched into a few details of what work he had done and had still to do. He refocussed as he heard his name mentioned. "Josh here has been a great help, I'm not sure what I'd have done without him."

"And how are you finding it, Josh?" said Kathryn, turning to him.

"Oh, delicious thanks!" said Josh, hastily swallowing his mouthful of shepherd's pie.

"Thanks" chuckled Kathryn, "But I really meant how are you finding life in the village? Are you managing to get out much? Do you like the beach?"

"Oh," said Josh, a bit disconcerted by his misunderstanding, "Sorry. Yes, we've been to the beach a few times, when it's not raining too much, and I had a wander round the churchyard too…" He stopped midsentence, suddenly unsure if he should be admitting to wandering round the graveyard by himself. Was it an acceptable thing to do? Owain, sensing his discomfort, hastened to put him at ease.

"We get a lot of people coming to wander round the churchyard and look at the church, tourists from all over the place, but it does have a fascinating history. Did you know it started life as a monastery in the seventh century founded by our local saint? He did a few miracles in his time, including, legend has it, bringing his cousin back to life after she had her head chopped off by a jealous suitor." He glanced quickly at Josh double-checking he was interested rather than disgusted. Satisfied with the expression of rapt interest on Josh's face he carried on. "He is buried under the chapel, the oldest bit of the church."

"The bit down the passageway?" said Josh, "I was wondering why there were so many different bits to the church."

"Yes, it can look a bit higgledy-piggledy at first" conceded the vicar. "That's the oldest bit, but there was a church here before that. It got burnt down a couple of times, first by the Vikings then later by the Normans"

Josh suddenly started to appreciate why the monks might have needed that secret tunnel to escape down to the sea.

"So, when was the current church built?" asked Darren curiously.

"In Tudor times," continued Owain "Around the fifteenth or sixteenth century. First the chapel was built as I mentioned, then they expanded it, and finally they added the tower. It was restored a bit by the Victorians, as was their wont, but they didn't mess it up too much, and it's still essentially as it was in Tudor times. Did you see our sun dial in the churchyard?" he asked turning to Josh again, who nodded. "That's really our oldest bit, dates back to the tenth century, way before the current building. Did you know it's actually a tide dial, so it measured canonical hours, showing the monks when their times to pray were, before they had clocks rather than more modern sundials which measure the hours of daylight, brought in by the Normans."

"Those monks sound like busy people," said Darren, "Didn't they have a farm as well?" He had been reading Josh's leaflet.

"Yes, they did indeed" said Owain. "Between the church and the sea.

"Is it true they had a secret tunnel from the church to the sea?" burst out Josh. He'd been waiting, hesitantly, for a good point to ask and this seemed to be as good as any.

"Ah, I see you've been reading our leaflet attentively" said Owain smiling. "That is the myth, but I'm afraid I'm not sure it ever existed. I've never seen any evidence of it and I'm not sure anyone else has either."

"Oh," said Josh, disappointed.

"I think it may still be there somewhere" said Kathryn, but Josh just thought she had sensed his disappointment and was trying to make him feel better. "Anyway, have you all finished? Would you like any more or are you ready for pudding?"

Josh perked up at the word pudding. He loved his food, but puddings most of all, though you wouldn't know it to look at him. His dad said he just grew upwards rather than outwards.

This time it was Kathryn donning the oven-gloves and producing a substantial apple crumble from the oven, while Owain rustled up a jug of custard. Bowls were produced and generous portions served.

"How much longer are you likely to be staying here?" asked Owain as they tucked in.

"I reckon I've got about another two or three weeks more work to do" said Darren, "It depends how many problems I encounter along the way. You never quite know what these old houses are going to turn up."

"Well, you know where we are if you need anything," said Owain, "Or if you have any questions about the area or the church, and I hope to see you again next Sunday."

The meal finished amicably with Darren answering questions about the rest of the family and their life outside Wales, whilst Owain and Kathryn in turn told of their grown-up children who both now lived in England. When he eventually glanced at his watch, Darren was surprised to see how late it was, and started to make moves towards leaving. With many expressions of gratitude, they regained their coats and edged out of the door, happily full. It had been a pleasant evening.

As Owain and Kathryn closed the door leaving them in the growing dusk, Josh noticed the rain had cleared up. His mind was filled with thoughts of the monks and secret passageways and he had a longing to see the beach again and wander about some more. "Dad, please can we walk back along the beach. It won't take much longer and we can walk off that pudding?"

"Oh, ok," replied his dad "But we'd better be quick. It will soon be pitch black and we might walk into the sea by mistake!"

There was still a small sparkling shimmer of orange on the horizon, where the sun had clearly quickly emerged from the rain clouds before setting. The waves looked eerie in the deepening gloom. Josh stared out at them, and that is when he noticed there seemed to be dark shapes moving through the sea, parallel to the shore. He peered harder into the dusk - they were too regular to be sea creatures, though they seemed to appear suddenly as if just swimming to the surface, then carry on floating out of sight. Something about the shape was familiar, cylindrical, and suddenly he thought he knew what they were - barrels! Perhaps there were some secret cider smugglers in the area!

His dad was a few paces ahead and he thought about calling him back to point out the moving shapes to him to see if he could make them out. Then he remembered his dad did not have his glasses with him and would probably just dismiss it as a trick of the light. Secretly, he preferred to keep this new mystery to himself. So, when his dad called "Hurry up Josh, it's getting darker," Josh took one final stare at the floating barrels, trying to commit every aspect of them to memory to puzzle over later, then shouted, "Coming", running after his dad and back to the cottage.

He was soon in bed, his stomach full and his mind whirring.

Chapter Eight

DOWN THE LANE

THE next morning the rain was gone completely and the sun shone between dappled clouds. Josh's dad still had a large amount to get on with, however, so when Josh asked about going for a walk to the beach he considered it a moment and said "I've still got a lot of this tiling to do, but I think you could be trusted to go for a walk down there by yourself this morning. You know where you're going and you've proved yourself to be sensible in helping me yesterday. What do you think, can I trust you?"

"Of course, dad!" said Josh, his words tumbling over each other, hardly daring to believe his luck, "You can trust me, I promise to be sensible. I know the way."

"OK then," said his dad, "as long as you come back in time for lunch and you stick around this afternoon to help me if that's OK. There's a few tricky bits I could do with an extra hand for."

"Of course, fine," said Josh, quickly gathering his hoodie and getting ready for a speedy exit before his dad thought better of it. "See you later, dad." He shoved his feet in his trainers without even bothering to unfasten the laces and ran out of the door. He remembered to slow down to cross the road with care, then settled for a cross between a slow jog and a quick walk down the now familiar path to the sea. He didn't meet anyone on the way and the only sound was that of bleating sheep in the neighbouring fields and the occasional moo.

The tide was partly out when he made it to the steps and climbed down to the beach. The sea looked somehow inviting, perhaps because of the mysterious sighting of the night before, so he decided to go for a quick paddle, pulling off his trainers, stuffing his socks into them and placing them safely high up on a rock far up the beach. He rolled his trousers up and picked a gap between rocks to paddle through into slightly deeper water. The sea was freezing, and he almost recoiled when his first toe touched it, but persevered for a few minutes. It was hard trying to avoid the rocks though, which were slippery with seaweed, and he eventually gave up and went back to the rock where he had left his trainers.

It was at this point he realised he had forgotten a towel. He wasn't quite sure if paddling counted as a sensible solitary activity in his dad's eyes, so perhaps it was best he had not provoked comment by bringing a towel. He decided he'd better just sit there for a few minutes till his feet dried naturally.

He sat and stared out to sea thinking about barrels. Where exactly had they been? There was no sign of them now. He glanced round the other way at the cliffs and the hidden building or mysterious old monks' farm that must be hidden behind them and allowed himself to speculate. Maybe the people from the farm were smuggling things in from the sea… From a ship - *was it too fanciful to think of it as a pirate ship?* - too far out to sea to see. What would they be smuggling? Possibly drugs or alcohol or something like that? He realised he knew very little of what people might actually bother to smuggle. There was no sign of anything now so perhaps he was getting too carried away. But he'd seen the barrels with his own eyes…hadn't he? While his dad had not seemed to notice.

He decided he needed to work out how to investigate more. He pulled his socks on over his now just slightly damp feet, thrust them into his trainers, and went for a haphazard walk along the beach before heading back to the cottage in plenty of time for lunch.

He carefully helped his dad out all that afternoon and the next day - it rained again so there was not much else to do. They worked hard together at all the tricky tiling jobs and really progressed the work on the bathroom. Somehow he felt like it was a good idea to build up credit with his dad, and keep in his good books in case he needed to call on any favours from him when he worked out how to explore further.

Chapter Nine

NIGHT TERRAIN

THE next morning Josh's dad announced he needed to get some more stuff so was planning a trip to the local town where he could pick them up in a hardware store. Josh welcomed the idea of a change of scenery and also thought a trip to the hardware store would be useful for the plans of his own which he had started to hatch.

They caught the bus at the usual stop. It was a cloudy day, but not too misty, so they got a good view of both the sea and the mountains on their way in. Josh checked he had his money in his pocket. Hopefully it would be enough to get him what he needed.

The shop didn't look that big at first, but then they discovered it had a sprawling basement. It was fascinating in a strange sort of way - all the different tools and odds and ends it sold. Josh had a pleasant wander whilst his dad spent time gathering all the things from his list. Whilst wandering though Josh was on the look-out for something in particular and eventually he spotted it on the end of a long aisle in the basement. Torches!

There was a whole range of them. Josh wanted one that was powerful, but small enough to fit in a pocket, and not too expensive. Eventually he settled on a medium-sized, green one. He flicked the switch to try it out. It was hard to tell in the bright shop lights, but the beam looked like it would be quite powerful in the dark. He was pleased to note it seemed to come with batteries included and went to re-join his dad who was on his way to the checkout.

"Is it ok if I buy this torch please, dad? I've got enough money," he said dangling his wallet in his other hand. He was hoping his dad wouldn't question his motives too much.

His dad just grunted, "That's fine," preoccupied as he was with manoeuvring his heavy basket onto the cash desk. "You go first."

Josh handed over the torch to be scanned, paid the man behind the till, and stuck it in his hoodie pocket (where, he was pleased to note, it fitted nicely) before helping his dad pack up into the two strong shopping bags they had brought with them and carry their purchases out of the shop.

They did a quick trip to the supermarket just down the road too to stock up on food. Josh made sure bacon went in the basket, before heading back to the bus stop. Thankfully this seemed to go from right outside the supermarket as they were now heavily laden. The bus arrived soon enough and they packed everything around them for the twenty minute or so journey back to the cottage. At least it was just a short stagger at the other end to get all the bags back inside, just in time for lunch.

As they were finishing eating their toast, Josh tentatively suggested going to the beach again.

"Actually, if you could just hold on a bit, Josh, I just need to get a couple of things done and then I'll come with you. I quite fancy going to have another look in those rockpools."

So, Josh had to wait impatiently for his dad, carefully fingering the torch switch in his pocket and trying to work out just what the next steps of his plan needed to be.

Eventually his dad downed tools and declared "I'm ready, let's go!."

Josh pulled on his trainers at super speed, his dad laced up his walking boots and slung his rucksack on his back and they headed out across the road and down the track towards the beach. The tide was part way out again and Josh tried to remember exactly where he had seen the barrels.

He was better prepared this time and had put his swimming shorts on under his trousers so he could have a paddle out towards where he thought the barrels had been. It was slow-going over the seaweed-slippery rocks, however, and hard to focus. There were no real landmarks in the sea to remember where those briefly-glimpsed barrels had been appearing from. Also, his dad was hard at work in the rockpools again and kept calling him over to see interesting specimens of shell and rock, as well as an elusive fish that swam off and hid each time he came to see it and, rather gruesomely, a dead fish's head, with large teeth staring at him out of its empty eye sockets!

Eventually Josh gave up and paddled back to the beach. He felt a bit annoyed with his dad for stopping him looking any further. He relented a bit though, conceding how much fun his dad was having peering into the rockpools. He had not seen him looking this animated for ages. As he sat shivering with wet legs perched on his lookout rock and wondering how on earth he was going to put his jeans back on over the top, what really made him appreciate his dad's presence was Darren's production with a flourish, as if it was some kind of magic trick, of a large fluffy towel out of his rucksack which Josh gratefully received.

Anyway, Josh realised he was not sure what it was he was trying to spot. Clearly whoever and whatever it was that had to do with the mysterious barrels, was not about to happen in broad daylight, especially with him and his dad in full view on the beach along with a couple of dog walkers.

He laid his own plans for later.

It was much later that evening when his dad was, hopefully, fast asleep, that Josh slipped down the stairs as quietly as he could, slipped a key into his pocket and his feet into his trainers, and let himself out of the front door, closing it carefully so it did not make too loud a sound. He had his torch safely stowed in his hoodie pocket, but could see a bit by a couple of dim street lamps - enough to find the start of the track down to the beach.

At first the excitement kept him going, but as he got further from the road and switched his torch on, all he could see was the small circle of light ahead of him, illuminating a tiny section of path, the rest of the world was in darkness, and it became slightly more daunting.

As he got closer to the beach, he started to worry that using his torch might alert anyone of his presence before he had chance to spot them, so, after a brief debate with himself, he turned it off. He stopped still for a moment and closed his eyes, listening to his quick heartbeat, before opening them again slowly and starting to see the glimmers of light in a world around him that he had thought was almost utter blackness. There was a crescent sliver of moon in the sky, and stars, lots of stars. The more he looked, the more he could see. There seemed to be many more here than he ever saw in his home city, but he knew that was just because there was much less light pollution here obscuring them. He found the three stars in a row that he knew formed Orion's belt, somehow finding reassurance in the familiar sight.

He set off again slowly. Now his eyes had adjusted to the dark. He listened carefully too for any sounds that could indicate that anyone else was near. All he could hear was a subdued *baa*, as if a sheep was disturbed in its sleep, and the continuous swish of the waves growing louder as he got closer to the beach.

Eventually the darkness before him started shimmering, and he realised he could see the faint moonlight glinting off the sea. He edged forward even more carefully now, feeling for the handrail at the side of the steep steps down to the beach. His hand found the cold metal and he used it to guide him forwards, cautiously feeling with his feet for each step. At the bottom he moved sideways, not wanting to move too far from the steps and lose them, though at the same time he definitely did not want to get caught by anyone else who might be using the steps.

He was probably only waiting there a few minutes, but it seemed like a long time, tensed and frozen, listening carefully and trying to make out anything he could in the darkness.

He realised the tide was high up the beach but there was nothing to see and nothing to hear, and he was starting to get cold. He made a mental note to bring his coat next time, and then started questioning if there would be a next time.

He hastily but warily retraced his steps along the path between the hedges till he was far enough away from the beach to dare to switch on his torch, then carefully followed the bobbing circle of light back to the road.

He took the key out of pocket and painstakingly turned it in the lock as slowly and quietly as he could. Eventually he heard the latch click. It was quiet but seemed loud in the darkness. He slipped inside, slipped off his trainers and put the key back where he had got it from on the dresser, slipping upstairs, back into his pyjamas and back into bed with relief.

Though he had been open to adventure, he discovered he was thankful that the trip had been so uneventful. Somehow though he still felt the urge to keep investigating – knew he needed to get to the bottom of the mystery of the floating barrels.

Chapter Ten

AIM

THE next day dawned cloudy but without actual rain. Josh's dad took a break at lunchtime and they went for a wander round the village together. Though it was a small village they were surprised to discover new parts to it. Down an unassuming side street off the main road, they found what looked like some kind of community building with a small playground and a basketball hoop. They messed around on the swings together for a short while and Josh decided to head back later by himself equipped with a ball he had seen under the stairs in the cottage to make the most of the hoop. His dad had work to get on with and he was keen to keep out of the way when he was not required to help.

Back at the hoop later as planned, he found he could not concentrate. The ball kept bouncing off the wrong side of the rim, as he was thinking about his plan of action. Maybe the sensible thing would be to forget about the barrels, perhaps even put it down to a trick of the light - but somehow he just couldn't do that. There was a feeling in his gut that the barrels were real and something else was not right, and he was determined to get to the bottom of it, or at least to try as much as he could. He plainly needed to go to the beach again that night. His dad had not noticed last time, and he was sure he could get away with it again. He was also sure that if he kept watch enough times he would spot another clue to help him solve the mystery.

With this newfound confidence, he threw the ball at the hoop one last time and it fell cleanly through the middle - he'd scored! He caught it deftly and bounced it back to the road then up the couple of streets back to the cottage, determined to see through a second night-time trip.

He took his coat this time and set off fractionally earlier. He wondered if he had arrived too late the night before, but could not risk leaving the house till he was sure his dad was asleep.

He still felt his heart beating loudly in his chest, but felt more certain of himself and what to expect. He knew now what he had calculated were the best points for switching his torch on (when he had got away from the road) and off again (when he was at the start of the last path to the beach). He again edged his way down the last path carefully, still very cautious not to trip over loose rocks, or fall down the steps to the beach. Again he managed to spot the glimmer of light off the waves, felt for the handrail and eased himself down the steps with caution.

He found his surveillance spot of the night before and stared out to sea. After a while he found himself yawning, his late night the night before catching up with him. He had to stifle a chuckle to himself - it was hardly the great adventure he had imagined. All was still and quiet except for the steady but gentle crash of the waves on the beach. He decided to go back. There was nothing here to see.

He had just re-joined the main track and was steadily following the small spot of light in front of him when suddenly he caught a movement just ahead out of the corner of his eye. He immediately clicked off the torch and stood stock still, frozen to the spot, uncertain what to do next. Who was there? Had they seen him? Could he evade detection by not moving or making a sound?

Who knows how long he might have stood there for, had he not suddenly realised what the moving shape was, as it gave out a plaintive *baaa* and jumped over the wall beside the path, back to join the other sheep in the field. He switched his torch back on and spotlighted its retreating back, flooded with relief.

He calmed his breathing and walked quickly the rest of the way back to the cottage. He still felt a bit shaky as he put the key in the lock and let himself in, placed the key back on the dresser and snuck back into bed. He had put his clothes over his pyjamas this time, partly for extra warmth in the slightly chilly night air, and partly so he could ease himself back into bed more quickly and quietly. He was glad of that now as he focussed on trying to settle down to sleep. He could smile about it after the event and couldn't believe how shaken he had been by an encounter with just a stray sheep.

The next morning he awoke feeling slightly calmer, perhaps lulled by the steady pitter patter of rain on the window. He yawned, reluctant to get out of bed after two very late nights but knew his dad would get suspicious if he stayed in bed too long. In general he wasn't a late riser. And there was an aroma of bacon drifting up the stairs. Since those first days in the cottage, breakfast bacon had become a rarer treat and he wondered what the occasion was.

He followed his nose down the stairs.

"Ah, there you are Josh," said his dad, just taking several rashers out from under the grill. "I thought I was going to have to eat all this myself."

"Thanks, dad. Smells nice," said Josh, wondering how he could work out the reason for the treat without directly asking. He was secretly speculating if his dad had just cooked it to lure him out of bed. If so it had certainly worked.

"Well, I thought I'd do us a Saturday treat," said his dad at last, carrying plates in one hand and the tray of bacon in the other. "Give us a hand carrying everything to the table would you?"

Josh picked up cutlery and bread and ketchup and carried them through in a bit of a daze. "Oh, it's Saturday!" he exclaimed quietly, "I'd completely lost track of what day it was."

It was true he thought, as he sandwiched his bacon between two slices of bread, added a dollop of ketchup and took a bite. All the days were starting to merge together. How long had he even been here for? A fortnight? Yes, it must be two weeks tomorrow. In some ways it seemed like forever, in others no time at all.

"I would have taken you out somewhere, it being the weekend" said his dad, "But I'm not sure it's really worth it in this weather." He jerked his thumb towards the window behind him, which rivulets of water were running down. "So, I think I'll crack on with some work if that's Ok. I'm sure you can entertain yourself."

"Yes fine," yawned Josh. "I feel like a bit of a lazy day anyway. Not much to do out there in this weather."

After he had polished off his breakfast and brushed his teeth, he settled himself in the armchair in the main room downstairs. He had a book he had brought with him which he was supposed to read for school, but after a couple of pages he lost interest. It was clearly too heavy going for his sleep-deprived mind.

Aimlessly, he picked up a newspaper from the dresser by the door. "What's this dad?" he asked, "Did you buy a paper?"

"Nah" said his dad, glancing up briefly, midway through rifling in his toolbox for an elusive tool. "That's the local free paper. It seems to get delivered every Friday. Have a read if you like; see if anything's going on."

Josh thought there was little likelihood of any organised events happening here that might interest him but started flicking through the pages anyway. He was on the verge of giving up and putting it down again when a strange headline caught his eye: *Ghost ship sighting claims.* Something about this new mystery captured his attention and he felt drawn to it. Could there possibly be any connection with his investigation? He read on. It seemed that some holidaymakers at a campsite, had claimed to have seen mysterious sightings of a ship late at night. They could just make out the ghostly shape of it on the horizon, with the white of its sails glimmering in the moonlight. It had just seemed to hover on the horizon, but when daylight came there was no sign of the ship anywhere. It did not meet the description of any in local harbours. The writer of the article seemed not to take it seriously and was quite dismissive of the whole affair, even going as far as to indirectly suggest that the holidaymakers may have been *having too much of a good time* to make reliable witnesses. Josh was not entirely sure what exactly was being suggested, but drew the distinct impression that no one but the two witnesses believed in the ghost ship.

But as soon as he thought that, he realised it wasn't true. He believed in the ghost ship. Well, he did not necessarily believe it was an actual ghost ship, but he believed something strange was going on and the ghost ship might just be a part of it.

He got the ordnance survey map from the dresser and opened it out on the floor. He checked the paper again, and then searched along the coast on the map with his finger till he found a name that matched. It did not take long. It was not far up the coast from where they were staying. He looked more carefully and found a caravan site symbol on the map. He had learned about ordnance survey map symbols at school and this was one of the easier ones as it bore an obvious resemblance to what it was there to portray - a small blue caravan symbol, accompanied by a triangular, tepee-shaped tent. This must be where the holidaymakers were staying, and it seemed to be less than a mile away westwards along the coast. This geographical closeness just reinforced Josh's sense that there was some kind of connection between the holidaymakers mysterious sighting and his own.

Josh glanced out of the window again, it was still raining heavily. There was no point even attempting to go out anywhere again today, or tonight.

He picked up his school book again and tried to read but his mind was whirring, trying to work out connections with all the tiny details which he was starting to see as clues in a mystery. Others might have dismissed them as mere fantasies, coincidences or tricks of the light but he just knew that wasn't right and he would try his best to solve it.

Chapter Eleven

STAIN

HAVING discovered it was Saturday, it came as less of a shock to Josh to realise the next morning that it was Sunday.

Over breakfast his dad asked him if he wanted to go to church again. "I was thinking it would be polite for us to go, seeing as how the vicar and his wife had us round for that lovely tea, but it's not compulsory, Josh."

"It's fine," said Josh, "I'd like to go."

Oddly enough, it was true. He took some kind of comfort from sitting within those whitewashed walls with the light streaming through the high windows, and the voices echoing in their bilingual litany. It felt peaceful somehow, even if he was not entirely paying attention to the meaning of all the words, just letting their sound wash over him and catching the odd phrase here and there. He recognised again some of the phrases he had noted the previous week, like "World without end…"

He also spent some time looking around at the congregation. There seemed to be a few more people there than the previous week including some different faces. Josh had chosen to sit by the dog tongs again, but he noticed a particular person sitting opposite them who he was certain had not been there last week. Josh could tell he was very tall, even when he was sitting down, and also very broad. The size of him alone was quite intimidating. *He might be a nice person anyway*, thought Josh to himself, but a sideways view of the man's expression showed it to be set and serious, and Josh determined to stay out of his way. Unfortunately for Josh this was easier said than done.

At the end of the service, they hung around briefly, waiting to talk to the vicar on the way out, who was deep in conversation with an old lady whose hand he was clasping. They exchanged brief greetings with a few people whom they recognised, and who recognised them from the previous week. One of them, a neatly-dressed lady in her sixties, turned out to be quite chatty, asking them how long they were staying and if they liked the beach, to which they gave their brief affirmative answers, but in reply, she said, "In that case you should meet Jac here. He farms right up to the beach and knows all about it,"

To Josh's horror, she turned around to summon the stern giant of a man towards her. "Jac, these people here have been enjoying the beach by you." Jac, still with a set, slightly sullen expression on his face, came towards them just as the talkative lady turned away to chat to someone else. Josh felt as if a thundercloud was looming and his stomach felt suddenly hollow.

"Oh, you like my beach, do you?" said Jac in a deep, thunderous voice that perfectly matched Josh's thundercloud image of him, "Well, enjoy it all you like but make sure you don't go in my sheep fields." And with that parting shot he strode past them, past the vicar and straight out of the door of the church.

Josh felt slightly shaken. So this was the mysterious farmer of the land by the sea and everything about him just heightened Josh's suspicions. He was not a man he would like to mess with.

The vicar came over then and greeting them warmly, asking them how their week had been. Josh's dad answered politely and asked questions in return. Owain talked about how they had been preparing for the church fete planned to take place in a fortnight's time, praying for good weather and hoping they would raise lots of money for a scheme they were setting up to help the local unemployed. "Will you still be here, then?" he asked.

"I'm not sure," said Darren. "It depends how the work progresses."

Josh suddenly realised he had not really thought about when he would be going home. Time here seemed endless. World without End. John would be coming home from Spain soon, and he had originally thought that was when he would go back too. But that would not give him long to solve his mystery. Would that be enough time to work out what was going on? He determined then and there that, however scary the farmer from by the sea was, and even if he was very likely to be involved in whatever was going on, he must aim to get to the bottom of this as soon as possible. He would go down to the beach again tonight for another look. Eventually he would spot something that would give him a clue. Perhaps tonight might be that night.

Josh realised again that he had completely drifted off from his dad and Owain's conversation, lost in his own thoughts, and had no idea what they had been talking about.

The vicar glanced at his watch. "Well I'm sorry but I'd better be rushing off again, my next service won't run itself. See you around the village no doubt, and I do hope you can make it to the church fete."

Josh's resolve weakened slightly as he once again let himself out of the cottage that evening after his dad had gone to bed, for his third night-time walk. He started to doubt himself, and if it was really worth going to all this trouble to work out what a few glimpsed oddities might add up to. But something in his gut was spurring him on, urging him that there was indeed a mystery to solve and he must try to get to the bottom of it. His legs disagreed and wobbled slightly in nervous apprehension. They still seemed to know their way instinctively to the beach, however, and carried him forward along the path once more following the bobbing circle of torchlight.

He hoped he wouldn't meet any sheep again and he switched his torch off earlier this time, partly anxious about the scary farmer and partly because he knew the way better now and could manage the gate to the last path in the dark. The moon seemed brighter tonight too. Again he edged forward steadily, putting his hand out just as the rail came within reach and the light glimmered off the waves.

After descending the steps he went off to the side again, and sat down on a little rock so he could focus on starting out to sea to see what he could see. The moon was definitely brighter he decided. He could see the waves more clearly, rather than just the faint gleam on his previous two night excursions.

And then he saw it, a brief flicker of something along the surface of the sea. It had been too dark and quick to see clearly, but he glued his eyes on the same spot to see if there was a repeat occurrence. At the same time, he glanced around the spot in question, desperately seeking some kind of landmark so he could remember where it was. He spotted quite a large rock jutting out of the sea just to the right of where he thought he had seen it, the kind that seabirds perched on during the day.

He followed with his eyes from the rock to the spot and suddenly, there it was again. A dark shape, that he was presuming to be a barrel, rapidly appeared, quite close to the rock and then drifted off to the west and out of sight in the lingering gloom.

He glanced back at the rock again. Were there any distinguishing features that made it special? As he stared at it, part of it suddenly moved. He let out an involuntary gasp, thankfully barely audible above the sounds of the waves. Rocks did not move, he knew that, so there must be someone out there on that rock, in the middle of the night, out to sea. That seemed to indicate to Josh that they weren't doing anything respectable, but were probably up to no good. What exactly were they up to though? And how could Josh find out?

He calculated how far out the rock was. The tide was quite high so there was no way he could get to it now. The best thing to do would be to carefully memorise the position of the rock as he had been trying to do, and to come back in daylight and explore it for clues.

The moon seemed to have gone behind a cloud and Josh was struggling to see anything else. He was also starting to worry in case he could be seen, so, he thought this was as good a time as any to make his escape.

He grasped the handrail and retreated back up the steps, along the path, through the gate, along the track past the sheep fields, through the other gate, alongside the houses, up the road and back to the cottage. His heart was beating hard and he still felt on edge, but also elated that he had finally spotted something, and had a clue to work on, hopefully the next day.

It was perhaps this elation that made him slightly careless, so he did not notice as he let himself carefully back in to the cottage that his dad had been touching up the paint on the doorframe by the front door, after Josh had allegedly gone to bed, before retiring himself. As he placed the keys carefully on the dresser, and gently brushed against the doorframe before hanging his coat carefully on the hook, he did not notice in the dark that he had left a tell-tale trail of paint on the sleeve of his coat.

Chapter Twelve

REMAIN

UNFORTUNATELY for Josh the next morning his dad did notice. The first thing he did when he got up was to check the section of paint he had touched up the night before, and noticed immediately that it was no longer perfectly smooth as he had left it the previous night, but slightly patchy and wrinkled, as if it had been touched when partly dried. *But how could that have happened*, thought Darren to himself. *No one's been in or out since he went to bed, unless…*

His father's instinct made him turn to the coats hanging on the hooks next to the door. He did not have to look hard. There was Josh's black jacket and there, on the sleeve, unmistakably, was a streak of white paint.

When Josh arrived downstairs half an hour later, bleary eyed from his night-time adventures and hoping for a good breakfast, he found his dad sitting stony-faced at the table, Josh's coat on the chair beside him. At first he did not understand what had happened, but he knew from the look on his dad's face that it couldn't be good. What was his coat doing there, he was sure he had put it back on the hook?

"Now, Josh," started his dad in a measured tone of disappointment. "How do you explain this?" He held out the paint-streaked sleeve of Josh's coat, and continued. "I only touched up that doorframe after you'd gone to bed last night, so how could this possibly have happened, unless you've been sneaking off in the middle of the night?"

Josh didn't know where to begin his defence, hastily trying to think of alternative explanations and as quickly dismissing them. My coat must have fallen off the hook? Then who picked it up again? No good. I must have brushed against some other paintwork earlier in the week. No use, his dad knew exactly which bit he had painted and when. Someone else wore my coat… Then who? And why did he bring it back again and hang it on the hook? It really was no good. Besides the look of dismay on his face had probably already given away his guilt.

"I..I…" he stammered, "I couldn't sleep. I… I just popped out to get some fresh air. I didn't mean any harm, honestly. I didn't get up to mischief. I didn't know you'd been painting the doorframe, or I'd have been more careful…" In his confused and desperate defence Josh was not really sure if he was in more trouble for sneaking out or for getting paint on his coat.

"More careful!" spluttered his dad, "More careful not to get caught you mean! Anything could have happened to you, wandering round in the middle of the night in a strange place!"

Josh judged it diplomatic not to remind his dad at this point that he had been there for two weeks and knew his way round perfectly well. Though he started to think that maybe that was not the point his dad was making. He quickly decided that the best policy was to stay vague about what he had done, apologise profusely and hope to be forgiven as soon as possible. He needed a quick pardon so he could go and explore that rock for more clues.

"I'm sorry dad, I didn't mean to worry you."

"Right," said his dad, "you're clearly not going to tell me what you were really up to, so you can stay in and help me work till I decide you're allowed out again at all, let alone by yourself." His tone softened slightly. "I thought I could trust you, Josh. You've really disappointed me."

"I'm sorry dad," repeated Josh, saddened by his dad's disappointment. He briefly considered telling him the whole story, but he couldn't risk him being dismissive of his suspicions, and he knew he would just get into a whole lot more trouble if his dad knew how far he had actually gone. So, he settled down, and accepted his punishment.

As soon as breakfast was over he put his and his dad's pots in the sink and started to wash up, without even being asked.

His dad looked at least slightly impressed when he came down to find Josh putting the last spoon on the draining board. "Thanks Josh," he said. "Now your next job is to try and get that stain out of your coat before it dries anymore. Turn the sleeve inside out and dab the back of the stain carefully with a bit of turps on a wad of kitchen roll. You don't want to be getting that on your fingers so you'd better put some of these gloves on. Keep dabbing and checking the stain till it's gone as much as you can get it to go. Then stick the sleeve in a bucket of soapy water to try and get rid of any remaining residue."

Josh carefully memorised his dad's instructions and started to follow them straightaway. He knew that his best hope of being released as soon as possible was to keep his head down and not put a foot wrong. He dabbed and dabbed at the back of the stain till it started to fade, and kept dabbing till it was hardly visible. Eventually, he decided dabbing was no longer having any effect and left the sleeve to soak in a bucket. He cleared up after himself and went to see what his dad wanted him to do next.

He kept on in this way, diligently doing everything his dad asked of him for all the rest of the day. He did not know how soon he could hope for a reprieve but went to bed early promising not to stir till morning. He would not have dared to go as far as the landing!

The next morning he got out of bed as soon as he heard his dad get up, hoping that if he worked hard today his dad might relent and let him go out to the beach. He did each and every job his dad threw at him, and tried to anticipate others before he was asked to do them. He started with washing the breakfast things again, chopped back weeds in the garden that were overgrowing the steps, dug up brambles, helped his dad fit a shower screen in the bathroom, made lunch, washed up again, sanded down the bedroom doorframes so they were ready for painting, and even put a couple of large potatoes in the oven so they could have jacket potatoes ready for tea. He was trying as hard as he could to be the perfect son and helper, trying not to answer back or be sullen or do anything that his dad could fault him on, but at the same time he was secretly planning in his head all the things he would do when he was granted his reprieve. He really needed to explore that rock, hopefully he could still remember which one it was, and work out what someone could possibly be up to out there in the middle of the night.

As Darren sat down that evening to his jacket potato heaped with butter, cheese and beans, carefully prepared by Josh who had even put a small cluster of cherry tomatoes on the side to make it a bit more colourful and healthy, he reflected on his son. He still was not happy at all that Josh had gone out in the night, for whatever reason, without telling him where or why he had gone. But he could not fault Josh on his dedication to make it up to him.

"OK, Josh." he began, "I'll give you credit, you've worked really hard today. Thank you for that. I don't know how much longer we'll be here for, so we had better make the most of that beach really. I still don't want you going anywhere without letting me know, day or night, but tomorrow you can pick what to do."

A wave of relief passed over Josh. He could have hugged his dad, but he was still a bit cautious about making a wrong move, so settled for a huge grin and, "Thanks, dad!"

"You've got one more job still today though," added his dad, putting his last forkful of potato in his mouth, "You can do the washing up."

Josh's face fell momentarily. Then he pulled himself back together but his dad had seen it and chuckled, "You do it so well!"

So, Josh dutifully piled all the dishes in the sink again, thinking of the next day and praying for good weather.

Chapter Thirteen
NO RAIN!

JOSH woke the next morning to a beautiful sunny day. As he lay momentarily in the bright shaft of light coming through the gap in his curtains, he had an idea. He was sure he had seen something on his visits to the village petrol station shop that might just come in handy.

When at breakfast his dad asked if he had decided what he wanted to do, he had his answer prepared. "I think I remember seeing a snorkel set in the shop. Would it be ok if I bought that please? I've got some of my money left. And we could try it out down at the beach."

It was a fairly modest request as they go, and his dad agreed readily enough, but insisted on coming with him. "We got through lots of work yesterday, so I think I can afford a bit of time off, and besides, I'm not sure how safe it is to swim out there. There may be tides trying to drag you away, I'll come with you."

Josh was a bit disappointed not to be able to go by himself so he could more freely explore the rock, but he was really just glad to be released under whatever conditions after his two days of hard labour. He needed to keep on his dad's good side still so could not afford to argue. Besides, his dad was always the one who remembered the towel!

He put his swimming shorts on under his trousers again as his dad put a few things in a rucksack and slung it on his back.

They went to the shop first, and there, as Josh had remembered, at the end of one of the rows, were a few items aimed at holidaymakers going to the beach. Buckets and spades in assorted colours and sizes, little paper flags on wooden sticks for sticking in the top of sandcastles, and some scuba masks, complete with snorkels. He quickly glanced at the price. It did not seem too bad.

He selected a blue one and took it to the checkout. In a minute he had paid, tucked his new purchase under his arm, and they were out of the shop and on the path down to the beach.

It seemed very familiar to Josh, and at the same time slightly strange to be going there in such bright daylight. His dad had made him wear his cap, but as the sun rose higher in the sky (or rather the earth turned to make the sun look further from the horizon) it got noticeably warmer. The sheep were out in force today too, baaing merrily in the fields beside the path and frolicking around in the grass. The steps were so easy to descend in daylight too! Josh hurried down them.

Despite the sunshine there was still only a couple of other people on the beach, strolling past walking their dog, and they were soon disappearing into the distance. There was a great view of the surrounding majestic mountains from the beach today too, lots of them were usually, at least partially, enveloped in cloud.

Josh had been worrying that he would not remember which rocks he had seen the barrels near and the person upon. He need not have worried. There were a lot of rocks but he had memorised its position so carefully that when he went and stood in his vantage point he knew it immediately. The tide was about halfway out, so he could paddle for a bit and then just swim the last few yards further to the rock. It should be relatively easy.

He started pulling off trainers, socks and trousers, as well as his t-shirt, so he was ready for a swim. "I'm just going to go out to that rock to try out my scuba stuff," he said to his dad, feeling like he still needed approval for every move.

"That's fine," said his dad, "Just don't go too far past that rock. It might suddenly get very deep."

Josh smiled to himself, the rock had been his aim for the last two days; there was no chance of him going beyond it, "Don't worry dad, I won't" he called. He wrestled mask and snorkel out of the packet, wedging the plastic wrapping into the pocket of his discarded trousers so it couldn't blow away. He tried it on. It took a couple of goes to adjust the strap so it fitted comfortably, and he was glad he had thought of doing it before he was treading water. He wedged it high on his forehead for now and started to walk down to the edge of the sea. The first touch of the water on his feet was still a rush of coldness, despite the sunshine, but he carried on, paddling carefully between the seaweed-slippery rocks.

Gradually the sea-floor seemed to get sandier and the water deeper and he pulled the mask down over his face, took the plunge and swam the remaining short distance to the jagged rock. He saw it was least steep on the right hand side and, after a couple of attempts, managed to clamber on to it. He remembered, however, that the barrels seemed to float off from the other side of it so he tried to scramble over the top. This proved harder than he had thought.

The rock rose up to a jagged peak and was wet, splashed by the waves, with its lower portions occasionally clothed with slippery green algae or dark squelchy bladderwrack. Eventually he had to concede defeat, climb back into the water and swim round the rock. There seemed to be no way to climb up on this side, but he clung on to the few crevices he could find and looked around for clues. He could not find anything above the surface of the water but he knew what he needed to do next. He fitted the snorkel to his mouth and plunged his head under the surface of the sea for a closer look, steadily breathing through the snorkel at the same time.

It was his feet which found it first. Steadily kicking out to keep afloat he found himself kicking against something solid and taut under the water. He turned his head and faced down in that direction to discover what seemed to be a rope, pulled tight and attached low down on the surface of the rock by a metal ring. This must be what the barrels had been attached to.

He swam under again for a closer look and found that rather than being knotted to the ring, the rope simply passed through it so there were two ends of the rope extending out into the sea, slightly apart from each other. He swam out a bit sideways from the rocks, following the ropes. They rose a bit closer to the surface, which could account for the way any barrels attached to them seemed to suddenly appear. The ropes extended for all he could tell indefinitely out into the sea, parallel to the shore. Josh thought it strange that no boats had discovered them. Then he reasoned that he had been to this beach quite a few times now and never seen a boat come in close to shore. It was a beach not much frequented and he guessed that if any holiday makers found the ropes, they would probably just dismiss them as connected with the local fishing industry. He had noticed bits of rope occasionally washed up on the shore, so it wouldn't seem too out of place.

Although becoming acclimatised to the water now, Josh was feeling a bit tired; he was not the strongest swimmer. He doggy-paddled back to the far side of the rock where it was possible to clamber up and have a rest. And a think!

He was still puzzled. If the barrels went off from this rock on the ropes, presumably some kind of pulley system, he still did not know what could be in them, who put them there or where they were going. One thing that was particularly puzzling was where they came from. It seemed a particularly complicated method of smuggling, if that's what it was. Boats could not easily get this close to shore to disembark any shipment into barrels, and it would be difficult to swim out here with any kind of contraband goods. Was it possible there were other clues the rock had not yet given up?

He noticed his dad was watching him and gave a cheery wave to signal that he was ok, before slipping into the sea again and going to explore the other facets of the rock he had not yet examined closely. First, he checked the side facing the beach, but found nothing out of the ordinary, before moving round to the side facing out to sea. Using his feet again, as they could reach furthest underwater, he explored the surface of the rock with them, once again clinging to crevices for support, and to stop him floating away. Again, this approach reaped success in the form of another metal ring. He put his head under the water for a closer look and was amazed to discover that the ring was not set in the rock itself, but into a square block of wood near the bottom of the rock. Excitement bubbled within him and through his snorkel. It could even be to some kind of trapdoor. Could this be the end of the mysterious tunnel he had long thought about? He really hoped it might be, and he longed to explore it but it was much too deep underwater to reach with his snorkel.

There was only one thing for it, he would have to come back at low tide and see if he could get down to it then.

He really was getting tired now, slightly chilly, and a bit wrinkly round the edges, so he swam back to shore and flopped down in the sun on the rock near where his dad was sitting, sifting through broken bits of sea shell in the sand. Though he quickly started to dry off in the sun, he was still grateful when his dad handed him a fluffy towel.

He felt he had made progress at last. The tunnel he had wondered about and no one else seemed to believe in did actually exist, and at the next low tide he would find out more. He decided he had better get himself a tide timetable.

Chapter Fourteen

BRAIN STRAIN

BACK at the cottage, he asked his dad where he could get a tide table from.

His dad immediately looked thoughtful, "I'm sure I saw one around here somewhere." He rummaged around in the drawers of the dresser and came back triumphantly with a small thin brown booklet which he presented to Josh. "Here you go."

Josh opened the booklet slightly nervously. He had never tried to read a tide table before. You didn't really need them in the city he was from.

At first it seemed to be just a confusing range of numbers and arrows, but gradually, with just a bit of help from his dad, he worked out the pattern and how to use it. Having worked out the principles he carefully worked out that the next low tide would be at 10.13 p.m. that evening. He was bitterly disappointed. There was no way that was going to work. His dad would not let him out at that time under any circumstances, and he dare not risk sneaking out again, even if his dad was in bed by that point which was unlikely. Besides even if he could swim or paddle out to the rock in the dark, he would not be able to see much. It would be much better to explore in daylight.

Reluctantly he carried on scanning the tide table. The following low tide would be at 10.40 the next morning. That should be perfect. The beach would not be too busy and he could explore freely. The only potential sticking point was whether his dad would let him out or not…which was currently an unknown factor.

He decided it might be worth broaching the subject sooner rather than later so when his dad asked, "Did you find what you wanted in the tide tables? What were you looking for?" Josh decided to plunge straight in.

"I was looking for when the next low tide is. I'd really like to explore some more of that rock. There are some really interesting bits low down on it that I'd like to investigate more." Having been caught out once Josh decided that telling as close to the truth as possible (without actually telling the whole truth) was probably the best policy.

"When is it then?" countered his dad.

"Tomorrow morning. 10.40 a.m. Do you think I can go then dad, pleeeease? I can come back and help you out in the afternoon with whatever you need help with."

"Oh, OK then," said his dad. "As long as you promise to be good, come straight back and don't go out past that rock. If you managed it today then you should be fine at low tide."

It occurred to Josh that he might have unwittingly given his dad the impression he was interested in the rock itself, but decided it was not worth disillusioning him. He was very interested in the rock, but for the secrets it might give up.

The next morning Josh was up bright and early. He'd packed his own rucksack this time, with torch and towel and snack and snorkel, in the hope his dad might let him go by himself. He was hoping he would but as his dad had not specifically said he could go by himself, did not want to rejoice too soon. But his luck seemed to be in. After breakfast his dad busied himself with jobs on the house and told him to have a good time. Josh did not need any further hints to take up this unspoken offer. He double-checked his bag, put on his trainers and left.

He had decided in any case that he should aim to be there a while before low tide, then he could carefully plan for the moment of lowest tide, and be ready to make his exit rapidly when the tide began to turn and come in again.

He almost skipped in his excitement going down to the beach. He checked his watch. It was just 10 o'clock. Arriving on the beach, he placed his things carefully on his usual rock and observed the state of the tide carefully. It was fairly low, but clearly receding lower still. He looked out and calculated that he could probably paddle out to the rock without any swimming at all. He was trying to decide whether to take his torch or not. It was supposed to be waterproof. It might arouse suspicions if anyone else saw him, but there was no one else on the beach. He decided to give it a go. It might come in useful.

Thus, holding the torch high above his head so it did not get splashed by the waves, Josh gingerly made his way through the seaweedy rocks and paddled the short distance to the large jagged rock. To his delight he could indeed paddle all the way.

He could now see that the top of the trapdoor was underneath an overhang of rock, completely covered in seaweed and still almost totally submerged though it was nearly low tide. This was what must be making it hard for anyone to spot. He bent down and felt through the seaweed, fairly quickly locating the metal ring that he had felt with his feet. It was too deep to see it clearly through the water but he felt round it carefully. Mainly it seemed surrounded by slippery slimy seaweed but there was one piece that felt different - a kind of soggy, wiry texture. He could not work out what it was underwater, so he pulled hard and brought it to the surface. As the water dripped from the white sodden thing in his hand he realised it was sheep's wool!

Josh was very puzzled now. What would sheep be doing out here. Surely they couldn't swim? And what would smugglers want with wool?

He pondered it all the way back to the cottage and still could not work it out.

The next day it was raining again, and Josh became bored. The seemingly unsolvable mystery was frustrating him. Every time he thought he was getting closer and finding more clues, he just found more issues to resolve. His dad had gone off to buy more paint, but Josh had opted not to go out in the torrential downpour, hoping to have time to sit and think, but thinking just made him more confused.

A loud thud disturbed his reverie, making him jump. He looked up and realised that it was something that had been posted through the door. He picked it up from the doormat. It was the free paper in which he had spotted the ghost ship in the previous issue. Now how did that fit in? Was the ship connected somehow? Or just an unconnected illusion? His brain was starting to hurt again now so he opened up the paper and starting reading it to distract himself, secretly hoping it might give him more clues, rather than just confusing matters further.

He skimmed through a few stories - shops closing down, a formerly famous footballer had passed away at the age of eighty-three, an elderly couple had been injured in a road accident. There did not seem to be much cheerful news this week!

Persevering he turned the page and a large photo of sheep caught his eye. He thought he might have had enough of sheep by now, with the frequent baaing in all the surrounding fields, but something made him start reading the article anyway. Perhaps it was the strand of wool he had found. Maybe it might tell him if sheep could swim or not. Further down the page he spotted a grainy black and white headshot of a familiar-looking face. He looked closer and suddenly realised it was the scary farmer he had met in church. He knew that farmer had been up to no good! He started reading the article again, more carefully, convinced that he was going to get to the bottom of this. Perhaps the farmer had already been caught and he would not need to do anything.

But as he read through the article it did not come out as he'd imagined. It seemed sheep were being stolen in the area by rustlers, specifically from the farm next to the sea. The farmer was being interviewed as part of the article - not as a captured criminal, but as a worried victim. No wonder he seemed stressed and stony-faced. Sheep were being stolen from his farm on a regular basis, threatening his livelihood. They seemed to be just vanishing, without any trace. No vans or cars or anything had been sighted on the gateway to the farm, where the farmer had set up CCTV. It was enough to make anyone look troubled.

Hold on a minute. Sheep going missing, vanishing into thin air, not going by road... Josh felt like everything was suddenly falling into place. The sheep were not vanishing into thin air, they were vanishing underground, down the ancient monks' escape tunnel, long thought to be lost, but in reality still there. And if they weren't going by road, they must be going by sea! That explained the bit of wool he had found by the tunnel entrance. So that was what was inside the barrels! Not guns or drugs or goods being smuggled in from the sea, but sheep! Sheep being smuggled from the farm out to sea. So where did they go then?

Josh felt his brain go into overdrive! He knew the direction they were floated on down the sea, along the coast... Presumably you could not keep a sheep for too long in a barrel. It would not be nice for the sheep, but he did not expect criminals to worry about that. But they must want the sheep to be in a resaleable condition at the end of it.

So, what was down the coast... The ghost ship! Of course, the barrels must lead to a ship, floating along on the rope pulley system. Josh felt he was on a roll! So, what if this ship was disguised as a ghost ship to throw people off the scent. Maybe so that it could not easily be recognised again if it, for instance, took on its cargo of stolen sheep from the end of the barrels' pulley system, sailed away down the coast to where it would not attract so much attention, and the sheep were then sold off illegally at a more distant farmers' market.

It was as if someone had just switched on a light in Josh's brain. Suddenly everything had just clicked into place and he could not think why he hadn't worked this out before. He must have been stupid. It all fitted together so well.

But what to do next, that was the question? Should he tell someone? His dad? The vicar? The farmer? No, he was convinced no one would believe him if he told them his theory. They would just dismiss it as the farfetched imaginings of a bored boy. At the same time, he knew that whoever was behind this must be stopped. He must try to catch them in the act. He needed help though. He could not possibly do it on his own.

He thought he might just have an idea. He would just have to find the right time to broach the subject. A new plan was coming together.

Chapter Fifteen

OBTAIN

THAT evening after tea Josh was sitting chilling on the sofa with his dad, and it was as good a time as any to bring it up.

"Dad, is it today John gets back from Spain?"

His dad sat back and looked thoughtful "Yes, it is, he should be getting back sometime this evening. I spoke to your mum on the phone when I was in town today."

Josh was about to interject but his dad carried on. "I suppose you'll be wanting to go back home now John is there…"

"Actually…" began Josh, seizing his chance, but his dad carried on.

"Look, I know it's not exactly been the most exciting place in the world for a lad of your age, but I hope you've managed to have fun at times, on the beach and in the sea, and you've been a real help to me, so thanks for that."

"Actually…" Josh tried again.

"And you've been here nearly three weeks now, which is what we agreed," continued his dad, "But there are a couple of jobs I was really hoping you could help me out with before we go. I'll only be here another week at the most, and I've been quite enjoying your company too."

"Actually," said Josh, pausing briefly for his dad to interrupt again before realising he was not going to. "I was wondering if, instead of me going back, John could come here and join us for the last few days. There are a few things I'd like to show him on the beach…"

"That sounds like a great plan," said his dad, relieved, "It would certainly save your mum worrying about John when she's trying to work. As long as he's not tired from his last holiday."

Josh thought this was a strange concept.

"We'll phone him in the morning and ask him, shall we? Maybe we could give him the weekend to recover and do his washing, or rather get it done by mum! Then, if it's ok with him, he can come on Monday. We'll stay till the following Saturday. Then I can get all the work finished off that I need to and we can join in the church fete before we go. Does that sound OK?"

"Sounds great," said Josh, though he was secretly wishing John could get there immediately. They would be hard pushed to catch the criminals by the next weekend, but they could certainly try. He thought it would look highly suspicious if it looked like he wanted to stay any longer than one extra week, so he tried not to let his panic show.

The next morning Josh was keen to phone John as soon as possible, but his dad made him wait a while, saying John must be tired as he'd only been due back late the previous evening. He was quite touched to see Josh's keenness to get his brother to come. The boys were not usually that close. He thought the time apart must have made Josh value his brother more. He must have really missed him.

At the appointed time they went to the payphone just up from the cottage. Josh's dad had insisted that he propose the idea of John coming to Wales to his mum first, just to reassure her that it was fine with both himself and Josh. But afterwards he promised to let Josh speak to John by himself.

Josh waited anxiously as his parents spoke to each other. He was worried John would refuse to come. He knew he had to convince him quickly of the urgency of the situation. Once his dad passed the phone over he began at once, very quickly. "Listen John, it's Josh…" but before he could get any further a familiar voice on the other end interrupted him.

"Josh, it's mum. Now before I put John on are you sure you're ok with staying there a few more days? I was worried you might be bored by now. Your dad could manage without you. You know, you can come home if you want to."

Josh had to change tack quickly. "Oh hi, mum. Yes it's fine. I'd like to stay; I really would." Again, he opted for sticking to a policy as close to the truth as he could get, without giving anything away. "There are some things on the beach I'd like to explore a bit more, and I'd really like to show them to John. Is he there? Is he going to come?"

"OK, Josh," replied his mum, amused by his keenness. "I'll get him now and you can ask him."

Josh waited impatiently as he heard his mum call to John. It seemed an age before he came to the phone and greeted his brother with a brusque, interrogative "Hello?"

"Listen John, it's Josh," he said launching back into his planned speech, his dad having retreated back to the cottage so he could speak freely. "I really need your help here. Please say you'll come."

"What, with the work on the cottage?" asked John, confused.

"No," continued Josh, uncertain how to explain and convince his brother quickly before the money ran out on the pay phone. "The thing is I think I've uncovered a mystery and I need your help, not with solving it as such, I think I've done that, but with stopping it. I can't do it by myself. I can't go into details now. I'll explain when you get here, please say you'll come?"

John, clearly impressed by the note of urgency in his brother's voice, was starting to soften "How long for?"

Josh was anxious to finally convince him. "Come down Monday, or as soon as mum will let you, and then you just need to stay till the following Saturday. Dad will be all done by then, and hopefully that will give us enough time…"

John was intrigued by the sense of mystery, and still feeling some residual guilt from his holiday. "Oh, OK then," he conceded. A few days in Wales might be fun. Josh certainly did not sound like he'd found it boring, and he was curious to see what all the fuss was about. "I'll persuade mum to let me come on Monday. I'll get my washing done first. See you then!.."

"Thanks, John," smiled Josh down the phone. "Oh, and bring your wetsuit."

The next day was Sunday and started drizzly. They went to church again, partly still feeling duty bound and partly drawn by the peace they both felt within those whitewashed walls.

Again, Josh relaxed and let the phrases wash over him. He noticed the farmer sitting at the far side of the church, and was still a bit apprehensive of him and so kept his distance. At the end of the service Josh made sure they hurried to the doorway where they could say a quick greeting to the vicar, along with a promise to be at the church fete the following Saturday, before making a speedy exit.

After another pub lunch, to celebrate what was to be their last Sunday there, the clouds had got less grey and more white and fluffy, and the drizzle had stopped and Josh was able to persuade his dad to go for a walk on the beach. As part of his slowly emerging plan to capture the criminals he needed to find some things to help him, and he thought the beach was a good place to start.

They went for a longer walk along the beach this time. Josh knew he needed to cover ground to find what he wanted and his dad, partial to more exercise, did not take much persuading. Josh kept his eyes peeled all along the shoreline. His dad presumed he was on the look-out for interesting rocks and shells and did not fail to point several out to him. Josh even picked up some specimens himself to show interest and distract his dad from his true purpose.

Eventually he caught sight of something likely looking in the distance and raced off calling out, "Back in a minute, dad." He wanted his dad to see as little of what he was up to as possible.

He ran up to what he had spotted washed up on the shore, hoping it was what he had thought it was from a distance. It proved to be quite a large section of strong, rope fishing net. Just what he was after. He bundled it up quickly and, keeping his back to his dad so he could not see what he held, ran to the top of the beach, above the tideline, and stuffed the net underneath a convenient large rock that was leaning towards the bottom of the cliff and creating a useful storage hole.

As he ran back to his dad, Josh hoped the net would keep safe till he could come back to retrieve it on his own, or with his brother.

He was planning to catch more than fish with it.

Chapter Sixteen
TOGETHER AGAIN

LATE the next morning Josh settled back into his seat on the bus and tried to relax. It had taken some doing, but he had managed to convince his dad that he could go to meet John from the station by himself, encouraging his dad in the belief that he would then not lose valuable time in his bid to finish work on the house by the end of the week.

It was a relatively straightforward process. Josh's dad had insisted on waving him off from the bus stop, only a stone's throw from the cottage anyway, and at the other end the bus stopped directly outside the train station. It had been dark when he had previously got the bus after he'd he arrived on the train, but he was fairly sure that he couldn't miss finding a train station.

He was looking forward to seeing John again. He was quite relieved that John could share the burden of the secrets he had discovered, and hopefully help him bring the sheep rustlers to justice.

He had studied the tide tables carefully over the weekend, by reference to the nights the newspaper article had reported the sheep being stolen on. He was fairly certain he had found a pattern.

Clearly the robbers could only operate when the tide was just the right height: too low and the barrels would not float through the tunnel; too high and they would not be able to get the barrels out of the tunnel and on to the pulley system. And clearly it had to be at that height at the right time of night, late enough to avoid curious passers-by, but early enough still to have time to get the barrels along the ropes to the ship and the ship safe into a port, and ideally its cargo discharged before morning, he would imagine, so as not to arouse suspicion.

He was becoming quite proficient at using the tide table now, and by Josh's calculations the next time the thieves would strike was this coming Friday. They were due to leave late Saturday afternoon, so it might be cutting it a bit fine, but it was their only chance.

He wondered how his brother would react to his story and plan, when he noticed a sign for the railway station out of the window and leapt up. This was his stop.

The little station seemed to have only two platforms, but he checked the board carefully and worked out the platform and arrival time of the train John should be on. His train seemed to be running five minutes late, which wasn't bad as train delays went, but made Josh even more impatient to see him.

As he waited, though, he started to fret. What if John dismissed his suspicions? What if he refused to help? But he dismissed these fears with a shake of his head. They might not be the closest brothers in the world, but John had a kind heart and was always up for an adventure.

Still, he felt his heart beat loudly in his chest as John's train pulled up onto the platform and he anxiously looked out for him descending from the train.

Eventually he spotted him, looking rather more suntanned than when he had last seen him, and waved.

John grinned and came towards him. They weren't really the hugging types but Josh was so pleased to see his brother he gave him a thump on the back in a kind of half-embrace. John might well have reciprocated but had a rucksack on his back and a cloth bag in each hand. "Give us a hand with these, will you? Mum was worried you and dad wouldn't be eating properly, so she's sent me with a cake, fruit and goodness knows what else. Anyone would think I was coming for a few weeks rather than a few days!"

Josh, happy to see his brother, was further cheered at the thought of cake, and gladly took the cloth bags off John so he just had his rucksack to manage.

The station was so small there were no ticket barriers on the way out, so Josh led the way up the stairs, over the bridge across the railway line, and straight out of the station at the other side.

"Come on, John, it's just round the corner to the bus stop and if we're quick we can catch the next one. I've got so much to tell you, I don't know where to begin…"

"What you mean, something actually happened in Wales?" asked John. "After all your complaints of how boring it was going to be!"

"Well kind of, and kind of not" said Josh. "If all goes to plan, I think it's about to get a lot more adventurous, if you'll help me… You see it started when dad and I walked back along the beach one night, after tea with the vicar."

"You had tea with the vicar!" spluttered John in disbelief "And that's where the excitement started?"

"He's actually a nice guy," countered Josh, "And his wife is great too, and they made us tasty food. But it was after we'd been to tea with them… Or maybe it really began before that when I heard about the mysterious tunnel…"

"Now that does sound more exciting!" said John, showing more interest. Though at that point the story had to stop temporarily as the bus arrived. They climbed on board the single decker together, Josh showing his return ticket and buying one for John, as his dad had given him money and he knew the name of their destination.

They hurried to the back seat together where they could continue talking in hushed tones without fear of being overheard on the sparsely populated bus. John was now eager to hear more, and Josh told him everything, from his first wonderings and suspicions to his Eureka moment where he had finally worked out what was going on.

John was a bit sceptical, but quite impressed with his younger brother's logic skills. "So, have you told dad?" he asked, though he was sure he already knew the answer.

"Of course not," replied Josh. "He wouldn't believe me; he'd probably just ground me again for having what he thinks is an overactive imagination. Besides, it's no use knowing how the sheep are being stolen, if we don't know who's doing it and have no evidence. We need to catch them in the act."

"And I suppose you have a plan how to do that," said John doubtfully.

"Well, actually…" replied Josh, lowering his voice even further to prevent being overheard by any other passengers, and going on to explain his tide calculations, how he was fairly sure when the thieves would strike again and his carefully thought-out scheme of how to catch them in the act, along with what further preparations needed to be done before then.

"Wow!" gaped John, when he had finished, feeling both astounded and slightly dubious, "You certainly have had a lot of time on your hands to come up with a plan like that."

"You will help me, won't you?" pleaded Josh, suddenly doubtful of his brother. "I can't do it by myself. That's why I asked you to come."

"And I thought you just wanted the pleasure of my company," joked John. "Do I have any choice? You seem to have got it all worked out." He softened slightly, still feeling some burden of residual guilt over his far flung sunny holiday with his friend, while Josh was stuck here in Wales. It was actually quite good to see his brother again. He hadn't realised how much he had missed him. "Of course I'll help, I can't let you go it alone little bruv."

Although he hated being called little, Josh broke out in a grin of relief, which quickly turned to panic as he looked out of the window and registered where they were. "Come on, quick, this is our stop."

Josh grabbed the two cloth bags, leapt to his feet and rang the bell, as John wrestled his rucksack back on. Then the two brothers hurtled to the front of the bus as it shuddered to a halt at the bus stop by the cottage.

"Here we are, John, welcome to Aberfawr!" Josh said with a smile as he led him to the cottage door, which he proceeded to thump loudly to get his dad to let them in.

His dad opened it within seconds, with a grin on his face to see John, and relief that Josh had completed his mission to meet him successfully.

"Hi John," he boomed, giving him a great big dad hug. "How was Spain? I expect you've been telling Josh all about it on the bus."

Josh felt a twinge of guilt for not even asking and glanced at his brother, who did not seem to mind.

"…But I'm afraid you'll have to tell me all over again. I want to hear all about it. We've had a nice enough time here, I think. The beach is pleasant enough, but hardly a lot to tell you about, is there, Josh?"

Josh and John exchanged glances.

"Anyway, come in, come in," their dad continued. "Put your bags down and make yourself at home."

Josh showed John round the small house, which took less than two minutes! In his keenness to invite John to stay, he had volunteered to give up his bed and sleep on a blow-up mattress on the floor for the last few days of their stay. When Josh showed John his bed, John could see what he had given up and was grateful to his brother, and therefore more determined, if he could, to help him in his madcap plan and to try and keep him out of too much trouble.

Josh was keen to show him the view out of the window. "Look, there's the big church opposite that I told you about, and if you just crick your neck a bit you can see the sea." As Josh pointed it out, however, both sea and clouds seemed to be getting ominously darker and greyer.

By the time they had got downstairs the clouds were blacker still, and by the time they had eaten the toast their dad had prepared as a late lunch for them, the heavens opened and torrential rain was pouring down.

Both boys grimaced out of the window.

Their dad smiled to see the likeness between them that was not always apparent.

"Oh, I was hoping to show you the beach," said Josh.

"Well, we can't go out in this," countered John. "We'd get soaked. Does it always rain in Wales?"

"Not always," said Josh, defensively. "We've had some lovely sunny days. Besides it wasn't raining on the way back from the station."

"You've changed your tune," laughed their dad. "You used to moan about the rain all the time!"

"Well, it did rain for all of the first few days I was here," said Josh.

"Anyway, nothing for it, you'll drown out there in that rain," joked their dad. "You'll have to go to the beach tomorrow."

Josh was not sure he could wait that long, but his brother had brought a pack of cards with him, so they passed the time playing games, eating his mum's cake, and occasionally helping their dad out when he needed an extra pair of hands for something.

The next day dawned cloudy, but thankfully dry. Josh and John promised to be sensible, and not argue, and their dad agreed that they could go to the beach together, while he finished off some jobs in the garden. They packed a couple of the homemade biscuits John had brought with him into a small tub which Josh put in his handy hoodie pocket.

"Do you want me to bring my wetsuit?" John asked Josh tentatively when their dad was not listening, eyeing up the grey clouds with caution.

"Not today, it's OK. We've got other things to do," replied Josh, and he lead John out of the cottage, past the church, and down the track to the beach.

John was full of questions now they were safely out of earshot of their dad. "You came down here in the dark? Wasn't it scary?"

"It's not too bad when you get used to it" replied Josh, nonchalantly. "Besides, I had my torch on for most of the way."

"Still…", said John, impressed by his brother's daring.

They were now walking on the part of the path that ran between the sheep fields. John eyed them suspiciously, as if they might disappear at any moment. "So, these are the sheep then? There still seem to be quite a lot of them."

"That's not the point John," replied Josh. "And keep your voice down, the farmer might be around somewhere, and I still think he's scary, even though I no longer think he's a dangerous smuggler. Come on, we're nearly there!"

They went through the last gateway and Josh ran ahead of his brother on the path between the high bushes, all the way to the top of the steps to the sea.

"There you go," said Josh, as if he was showing off his own beach.

"Yeah," said John eyeing the vast empty expanse of sand and the distant mountains with their tops in the clouds. The beaches in Spain had been crowded with barely any space to move. "Looks cool. Does no one else ever come down here?"

"A few dogwalkers, their dogs, the very occasional tourist and…" Josh paused, then added in an undertone, "Sheep rustlers! Who we're going to catch! We just need to find things to catch them."

John hoped his brother was not being too naïve. "And what exactly do we catch them in?" he asked, confused.

"Nets!" said Josh triumphantly "Great for catching anything! I've found one already and stashed it away, but we could do with another couple at least. They're always washing up on the beach.

We just need to walk along till we find some. It should be a lot easier now without dad watching over my shoulder all the time."

So, they strolled along the beach together, John occasionally stooping to examine an interesting rock or shell. It made such a change to be on this wild, windy and spacious beach after the stifling heat of crowded Spain. Secretly, he wasn't sure that he didn't prefer it here. He was uncertain about mentioning it in front of Josh, in case it was still a sore subject for him. They had had so much else to talk about, it hadn't really been mentioned between them since John's arrival.

"You know there were hardly any shells in Spain," John began tentatively, "A lot of sand, but not much else. Except a lot of people!"

"Ah you see, Wales wins every time!" laughed Josh and ran off after something he had caught sight of that he was hoping might be a net. When he got closer, he saw it was just a rope, but he still thought it might come in useful, so he picked it up, coiled it round on itself, then pulled a cloth bag out from his hoody pocket and placed it inside.

"Is there anything you can't fit in that pocket?" grinned John. Then, looking closer, "Is that mum's bag I brought with cake in yesterday? She'd kill you if she knew you were using it for dirty stuff off the beach."

"Needs must," said Josh, focussed on the task in hand. "I needed a strong bag. Besides, it will wash."

A little bit further on, Josh struck lucky again, with a large piece of fishing net washed up on some rocks. It was even a bit big for the bag, so Josh stashed it under his arm. Not much further on and he was able to show John the one he had hidden away when he was with his dad. He ran ahead and pulled it out from behind the rock with a flourish "Here's one I found earlier!"

"How did you know it would still be there?" asked John, amazed, in spite of himself.

"Oh, I just knew; I hid it well," said Josh, nonchalantly, secretly relieved, both that it was still there, and that he had remembered where he had hidden it. "Here, you can carry it now," he said thrusting it at John, who was too bewildered to do anything but obey. "I think we still need at least one more. Let's keep looking," and he ran off up the beach towards the next corner.

John followed at a more leisurely pace, enjoying the windswept landscape. As they were rounding the corner, he glanced back and discovered the cloud was starting to lift from the distant mountains, which towered majestically up into their mist-swirled tops.

They walked on quite a bit further, and were about to turn around and give up to try going in the opposite direction along the beach, when John spotted something right by the edge of the waves and went to investigate. He got his feet wet grabbing at the dark shape sticking up out of the waves, but it was worth it for the strong black polyester net he triumphantly pulled out of the sea, one-handed as he was still holding Josh's net in his other hand. This net had finer mesh this time, but looked strong.

"Good enough for you?" grinned John.

"Looks great. Good spot," conceded Josh, managing to stuff it into the cloth bag with the rope. "I think it might be biscuit time now."

John had forgotten all about their mum's biscuits in their little container in Josh's pocket, so it was a lovely surprise to be able to sit higher up on the beach (the tide seemed to be coming in) and enjoy them together.

Then, energy renewed, they were ready for the long walk back along the beach, encumbered by a net each and the bag, and being quickly chased by the advancing tide.

Chapter Seventeen

DRAIN

THE next day, Josh had a greater challenge in store for John. He had been consulting the little brown tide booklet again, and calculated they wanted to be on the beach by about ten in the morning, just half an hour before low tide. John had handily brought not only his own wetsuit, but Josh's too. For some reason, Josh had not bothered packing it when he first came to Wales. Probably a combination of a lack of enthusiasm for his trip, the fact it was getting a bit small for him, and generally that it was bulky and he just could not be bothered to carry it. So he was extra grateful to John for making room for it in his rucksack.

Josh had to squeeze into it but managed, just. John put his on too. Then both boys put their clothes back over the top. Their room smelt slightly of salt water, due to the three nets and rope they had managed to hide under the bed the day before when their dad was still out working in the garden. They were really hoping it was not strong enough for their dad to notice. They did not take any more biscuits this time - they did not want them to get wet - but Josh packed a towel (he was learning from his dad) and his snorkel and mask set in a wet kit bag, also brought by John. He thrust some money in his pocket as well. They had promised to be back in time for a late-ish lunch so they could then help in the afternoon with any jobs their father was struggling to do single-handedly.

"Right," said John, as they came out of the cottage and round the corner on to the road. "What's today's challenge?" It was hard to discuss plans inside the house without their dad overhearing, even in their room, as the wall between theirs and their dad's room was paper thin.

"First," said Josh. "We have a bit of shopping to do. "You'll be needing a mask and snorkel too, my treat."

He led John to the petrol station shop on the edge of the village and went straight to the end of the aisle selling beach goods. He got John to pick a colour quickly, paid for it at the checkout and they left the shop again. He glanced at his watch, forty minutes till low tide. "Let's hurry down to the beach now." He bundled John's new snorkel set into the bag, slung it over his shoulder and led the way down the path and track to the beach.

"So, I gather we're going to do a bit of diving. Whereabouts exactly?" asked John.

"Out to the rock and then into the tunnel, hopefully," replied Josh. "I haven't been in there yet, but we have to prepare for it being at least partially flooded, even at low tide. When the thieves use it, we know it has to have enough water in to float a barrel, but enough air they can still breathe if needed. We need to be prepared for all options. Also, we need to explore it now, at low tide, so we can work out our way around it, and where it goes, find out how exactly the sheep stealers are using it and decide where the best place is to catch them!"

Though he was trying to seem outwardly confident in front of his brother, Josh was feeling a mixture of excitement and trepidation. It was a big adventure, but who knew what they might find down that ancient tunnel. He was just banking on the fact that the sheep rustlers would not be down it while it was broad daylight outside, and hopefully no one else would notice them either.

When they got to the beach, which was fortunately deserted, they took their outer clothes off quickly and stuffed them in the bag which they hid behind a rock at the top of the beach under the shallow cliff. They agreed they did not want a seemingly abandoned bag to attract attention or suspicion. Nor for their clothes to go missing!

It was slightly brighter than the previous day, but not that warm, and they were glad of their wetsuits as they picked their way carefully across the slippery rocks towards the far out sea. They each had their mask and snorkel and Josh had his torch. He was glad he'd bought a waterproof one! The water in the rock pools was chilly and, as they watched their footing, they caught sight of a small fish, flashing quickly out of sight into the sandy depths of the pool.

Josh pointed out the rock to John and they paddled there with ease. Josh was now very familiar with the rock and showed John which side it was possible to climb up and which side not. What they were really interested in though, was hidden just beneath the surface of the sea, underneath the overhang of the rock. It was the trap door! John was almost as excited as Josh had been when he discovered it. Even though Josh had told him it would be there, John did not like to admit, even to himself, there had been some niggling doubts in his mind about his brother's story. To be fair, it did sound rather far-fetched, so who wouldn't have had doubts? But, finally, here was some evidence that there were a lot more mysterious aspects to this quiet beach than at first appeared.

Josh was really hoping that, as the thieves seemed to use the tunnel on a regular basis, the trapdoor would not be too stiff. He bent down and extended his arm into the water to grab hold of the metal ring. He tugged, but it did not budge. "Here let me have a go," said John, hoping his slightly longer arm might do the trick but it still would not budge.

"Well, I guess we'd better try together then," said John. Josh took hold of the ring too, and they heaved, and wriggled, and pulled, and the door suddenly shifted forwards, taking both of them by surprise, and they burst into fits of suppressed giggles. They were glad of the bulk of the rock, hiding them on their supposedly covert surveillance operation!

"Well, let's see what's down there," said Josh, putting on his mask and snorkel. John did likewise, not knowing if his hands shook from fear or excitement.

"I hope those monks had spacious tunnels!" said Josh.

"What are we going to do with the trapdoor?" asked John, holding the edge of the door in his hand, "We don't want to leave it open to attract attention, or flood the tunnel, but, if we close it, we might not get out again, if we need to come back this way?"

Josh considered this briefly. "I know, let's wedge it ajar with a rock. There must be one around here somewhere." He felt around on the sea floor with his feet "Here's one! It's a good job this beach is so rocky!" He manoeuvred it with his feet so it was by the edge of the tunnel entrance and would stop the trapdoor from closing by a few centimetres, enough not to be glaringly obvious, but a big enough gap for them to be easily able to push it open from the inside. "We'd better get going. The tide will start to change soon, and I want to be back out again before it gets any deeper than it is now."

He took his torch and shone it in the tunnel, but could not see a lot past the initial wall of water. There was a narrow air space at the top though so he could still breath through his snorkel. "I'll go first, you wedge the door ajar behind you" he said to John, and before he could think too much about it, or John could argue, he took the plunge and dived into the tunnel, his torch gripped firmly in his hand.

The passage seemed to slope downwards initially, and Josh worried it would just get more full of water, but after a few metres he sensed there was a larger gap above the water and raised his head up carefully, so as not to bang his head, and discovered there was enough airspace to breathe without his snorkel.

He was relieved to see John surface behind him. They gave each other a tentative grin then slowly made their way forward and still downward, pushing the water behind them with their arms to give them extra propulsion.

The tunnel looked like it had been carved out of rock, and was just wide enough to fit a person, or barrel, and tall enough for a grown man to walk only slightly stooped. Josh found his head did not quite touch the ceiling, but John had to be careful as there was a very narrow gap between his head and the rock above at times, and sometimes no gap at all.

Josh shone his torch at head height and the yellow light reflected eerily off the black water. As they carried on forward slowly but steadily, the depth of the water lessened and the height of the airspace increased. Their pace also quickened as they were paddling up to their knees, rather than floundering in deep water.

Suddenly Josh noticed something as they rounded a curve in the tunnel. "Hold on a minute," he said to John.

"What's up?" said John.

"The light looks different ahead. Let me try something" replied Josh, and he turned his torch off, seemingly plunging them into darkness, but, as their eyes adjusted to the gloom, they saw some hazy light up ahead. But where was it coming from?

Josh took a tentative step forward towards the light source. "I think there might be a hole in the roof. Let's get closer and have a look. I might need to switch my torch back on for a bit though." He did so they could progress more quickly and a bit further on, Josh's torch highlighted a pile of rocks on the floor. They looked above it and saw light coming through. Clearly the roof had collapsed here at some point at one side. Josh switched off the torch. Although some light coming through it looked like the hole was partially blocked from the outside.

"Hey, look at this," said John, "Shine your torch over here a minute."

Josh swivelled round in the enclosed space, switched on his torch and shone it in John's direction. John was clutching eagerly at the wall of the tunnel, where a knotted rope hung down from the ceiling. "Look," repeated John, "Someone must have been here recently and got out up there," he pointed to the gap above, towards which the rope spiralled upwards. "Do you think we should take a look?"

"I'll go," said Josh, making a quick decision, "I'm more likely to recognise where we are than you, and the rope is more likely to hold my weight." Before John could disagree he handed over his torch and scaled the knotted rope, which was harder than it looked with wet and slippery hands and feet.

Once at the top, he held on to the rope with one hand and parted the branches that seemed to be covering the hole with the other. Clearing a small space he poked his head through, closing his eyes involuntarily in the bright light after the torch-lit gloom of the tunnel. He opened them again and gave an involuntary squeal, quickly stifled, as he found himself face to face with… a sheep!

"What is it?" John called anxiously from below. "Are you OK?"

"Yes fine, sorry," said Josh recovering himself. "Just a sheep gave me a shock! Give me a minute."

He quickly observed all he could of his position, the equally startled sheep having retreated to a safe distance. He swivelled himself carefully around, still clinging carefully to the rope, wanting to clutch at the grass with his other hand but uncertain what was strong enough to hold him, and not wanting to leave any traces behind of his presence. He carefully established which direction the sea was, estimated how far away it was, swivelled a bit more so he could see the church in the opposite direction, looming quite close, and calculated roughly whereabouts they were. He also studied the surroundings of the hole itself. There was a large rock lying flat nearby, and also a bush. Whether the movements of rock or bush roots had caused the tunnel roof collapse, and whether that had occurred recently or hundreds of years ago he could not tell. The rock seemed to partly hide the tunnel collapse and, again, whether than was deliberate or accidental he could tell. It was also partly obscured by the bush, but it did look like some branches had been placed over the remains of the hole next to the bush, perhaps partly to hide it from view, perhaps just to stop sheep falling down it.

He was conscious that he was in the middle of the field belonging to the farmer, who still scared him, even though he was now convinced he was a victim of the rustlers rather than a perpetrator, and retreated back down, pulling the branches over the hole again, observing as he did so that it was just big enough to fit a person down, or a sheep.

He slid back down the rope carefully and reported to John what he had seen. "We're in the middle of the farmer's sheep field, closer to the church than the sea. It looked like the roof's collapsed in by itself at some point, goodness knows when. It may have been naturally obscured by a large rock and a bush, which may have prevented its discovery. Though I guess no one goes in the field except sheep, so as long as they don't manage to fall down there, there's no reason to think it would be discovered."

"But how did you get your head through then?" asked John.

"Well, I'm not sure if it's been widened or what," responded Josh, "but there's a part of the hole not obscured by bush or rock and it's been covered over with branches. It looks deliberate, but for all we know the farmer could have done it himself to protect the sheep."

"So, you think this is how the thieves are getting to the sheep?" asked John, his belief in Josh's theory becoming more and more firm by the minute.

"I'm certain of it," said Josh. "One of the key features mentioned in the paper about the thefts was that, despite CCTV on the track leading down to the farm from the road, there was no sign of a truck, a van, or even anyone notable on foot arriving at or leaving the farm." A sudden thought struck him, "I hope it didn't pick me up on the CCTV!" He paused, then dismissed his fear, "Nobody could understand how sheep could just disappear by themselves!"

"Till now," interrupted John, grinning in the gloom.

"Till now," agreed Josh. "They could come along the beach, slip smoothly into the tunnel without anyone noticing like we did."

"Well, I'm not quite sure you could describe our entrance as smooth," chuckled John.

"Well, maybe not," continued Josh, "But they'll be more practised than us. They just need to come along the tunnel to here, pop up the rope and capture a sheep. I would have thought that would be easy enough in the dark when they're sleepy. One practically walked into me!"

"And then they bundle the sheep into barrels, poor things, float them down the tunnel and off over the sea on their pulley rope system to their secret ship, and get away without anyone ever seeing them," finished John.

"I was going to say that!" said Josh, slightly indignantly, "But, I was just wondering where the barrels come from…"

"Over there" said John, flashing the torch which he still held, "I had a look around down here whilst you were looking round up above." In the torchlight Josh could see that the passage widened slightly up ahead, and, stacked at the side, were about six large wooden barrels, each just about big enough to hold a sheep. "I'm guessing they push a couple of sheep-filled barrels at a time along to the exit by the rock, where maybe an accomplice helps transfer them on to the sea pulley system. Then when the empty barrels come back they bring them up the tunnel again and fill them with more sheep, or leave them ready for next time."

"You're starting to think like me," smiled Josh, then glanced at his watch with a worried expression. "The tide will be starting to turn. We'd better get a move on. I don't fancy going back through the rock entrance if it gets too deep. A gentle paddle like we're doing at the moment suits me fine. Neither do I fancy going through these sheep fields. The farmer might be around and mistake us for the thieves. It doesn't bear thinking about what he might do then. What do you say to going further through the tunnel towards the church and seeing if we can find the exit there?"

"I say lead the way!" said John, handing the torch over, "But be quick about it in case there's no way out that way and we have to go back out of the rock entrance again."

"Come on then!" said Josh, with a renewed sense of adventure, shining his torch past the barrels and setting off at a quick paddle.

The tunnel seemed to narrow, but slope uphill slightly, and the water got shallower till eventually they were not really paddling at all. Also, the walls of the tunnel seemed to gradually become less rocky and more earthy. Eventually the passage curved round a corner and stopped abruptly. Josh had to stop himself from walking into the wall of earth ahead of him, and John had to stop himself walking straight into Josh. Having stopped dead in this way, they looked around them.

"Do you think the end of the passage has just been buried?" asked John, pessimistically.

"No," said Josh, inclined to be more hopeful, "This wall doesn't look like a tunnel collapse, it's quite vertical, almost as if it was deliberately the end. Besides, we must be nearly at the church by now." He shone his torch on each of the walls in turn, and then turned the beam upwards. There, above their heads, it shone on wood. "Look!" said Josh triumphantly, "It must be a trap door!"

"Great," responded John excitedly, his eyes shining in the torchlight. Then he added more despondently, "But how do we get out of it?"

"Erm…" said Josh thoughtfully, "I guess the monks must have been always entering this end to make their escape, so they could presumably just open the trap door and lower themselves down, without needing to worry how to get out of this entrance again…"

John grinned "You always have a plan, don't you? Come on then!" He steadied himself directly underneath the trap door while Josh jumped up on to his back, which was trickier than you might imagine in the narrow tunnel.

"Hold on to me tight, please," said Josh.

John gripped his legs firmly as Josh took advantage of his new elevated position to push upwards with his hands flat against the wood. He had not expected it to move at all on his first attempt, but it did seem to shift slightly. "Ok, I'm going to try with my shoulders", he said. "Brace yourself," and he barged against the trap door with his shoulder and all of his might. And it shifted!

The stiffness of the entrance at the rock end must have been caused by it being under water so much. This end was an old, heavy trap door, but seemingly an ill-fitting one, with just a few stems of weeds holding it down, which had snapped under Josh's sustained pressure. He managed to move the trapdoor slightly to one side and leave a gap. Another shove and the trap door was further to one side leaving a gap wide enough for Josh to scramble through.

He had a quick glance around. There was a lot of undergrowth here, bushes and ivy. He peered out quickly under a branch. There was the church, very close by, and, even nearer, a flash of red disappearing into the adjoining bush. It was the robin! They were in the overgrown corner of the church yard. He wondered if the monks had been the first to neglect it, the better to disguise the entrance to their tunnel. But he did not have time to ponder on it. He lay down flat amongst the undergrowth and extended both arms to John in the tunnel below, "Come on, I'll pull you up."

After a bit of heaving from Josh, and jumping and grabbing earth from John, they were both safely above ground. Josh carefully lowered the trap door back into place and covered it with the undergrowth again. "Now is not yet the time to reveal its continued existence, I think. We might need to use it as part of our plan. I think this entrance will be a lot easier to access than the one by the sea, and we're much less likely to meet the crooks at this end."

John was exhausted from his climb out of the tunnel and lay flat on the floor.

"Come on John, no time for laying around I'm afraid, we'd better go get our stuff back from the beach."

"Oh yeah," groaned John, "I'd forgotten about that. Do we both need to go?"

"I think so, sorry," replied Josh. "Two of us wandering round in wetsuits looks a bit less suspicious than one of us on our own, and I think we both need to wash some of this mud off before dad sees us."

They looked down at themselves. They were mud-splashed all over, but their feet especially were covered in black gunk. "At least it looks like we're wearing shoes!" laughed Josh.

They tried to look as inconspicuous as they could on their way back down the path to the beach, but were very self-conscious that they were two muddy, barefooted boys in wetsuits with snorkels and a torch. Fortunately, the only person they met on the way was a distracted dog walker who was being pulled along by an over-excited labradoodle and did not really seem to notice them. They were grateful for the strip of green grass that ran down the centre of the track to cushion their feet. The last narrow path that led to the steps down was a bit stonier, but, grateful to be nearly there they just hurried on to the steps and down on to the sandy section of the beach which felt blissful to their sore feet.

"Come on," said Josh, "We promised dad we wouldn't be too late back. We'd better wash off this mud."

They picked their way carefully over the rocks and paddled out till they could immerse themselves more easily, swim briefly, and rub at their legs to get the mud off. They were just heading back towards the shore again when Josh remembered something. "Hold on a minute John, I just need to do something" he said, swimming off towards the rock.

John waited a moment then swam after him, hoping he was not going to attempt to go in the tunnel again. He arrived to find Josh diving under the water, then re-emerging triumphant with a rock in his hand. "Just moving this out of the way that we left blocking the door open," he said with a grin, tossing the rock to one side. "It would be a bit of a giveaway if we left it there."

"Good thought," replied John, once more impressed by his younger brother's planning, as they swam, then paddled back to shore together.

They retrieved the bag from its hiding place and towelled themselves down as quickly as they could. They were running close to their dad's deadline. Pulling on their shoes gratefully they headed back to the cottage for a very late lunch and to help their dad.

Chapter Eighteen
CAMPAIGN

THEY worked hard that afternoon to help their dad, partly to counteract the effect of their tardy return.

The next day they helped too. There were a lot of fiddly finishing off bits to do before their departure on Saturday and their dad was determined to leave everything as perfect as he could. He sent them scurrying around the house, fetching tools and equipment, wiping things down and so on. Josh and John did not mind. They were as ready as they could be in their plan to catch the sheep stealers and could think of nothing else they needed to prepare in advance, and Josh was convinced in his calculations that they would not strike again till Friday, the next day. Besides, it was pouring with rain and the damp grey gloom outside was not very inviting. They preferred keeping busy to keep their minds from the coming adventure. Josh felt a lot of trepidation, hoping his plan would come off, and John, though determined to stick by his brother, who had proved himself an expert planner, was starting to worry that they had forgotten some essential detail.

They dared not discuss any aspect of the plan in the small house for fear of being overhead all that day and night, but Friday morning they reached the stage where they needed to go out and go over the final finer details together. It was still a bit gloomy, but not raining outright, and Josh asked if he could take John for a walk in the churchyard to show him the robin's nest, promising to be back within an hour to help with any remaining jobs and packing.

John raised his eyebrows behind their dad's back, but did not dispute this sudden interest in ornithology. Their dad did not query it either, having heard Josh talk about the robin with enthusiasm after his last visit, and agreed they could go.

John waited till they were over the road to raise his eyebrows. "What's all this about a robin?"

Josh explained. "I decided after dad found out about me sneaking out in the night that it worked best to tell as near to the truth as we can get away with, without giving ourselves away." He grinned at John "That robin, or rather a family of robins, happens to live very close to our newly discovered trapdoor. Dad likes us to show an interest in birds, and I thought we really needed to just get out for a bit, check over the trapdoor again and finalise plans for tonight."

Josh led John to the far overgrown corner of the churchyard, stopped suddenly near the wall, and said, "Just wait and watch a minute please."

"Just what exactly am I waiting…"

"Sssshhh," interrupted Josh. "You'll see."

So they waited, John impatient and perplexed, Josh calmly confident, and in about thirty seconds a flash of red appeared and alighted upon the wall, a pink worm wiggling in its beak.

"A robin!" gasped John in amazement, "There really is a robin!"

The robin ignored him and dived into the bush from which a series of exciting high-pitched cheeps emerged as the chicks fought over the worm.

"Aw, and it's got babies," John continued, in spite of himself. He was further amazed when a second robin appeared on the wall, the female this time, complete with second worm, waited for the first bird to emerge and then flew into the nest to even more cheeps.

"THEY have got babies," said Josh, correcting him, "who are constantly hungry, so they're constantly feeding them. And now when dad asks you about the robins you can respond convincingly and say you saw them. Now, let's go have a look at this trap door."

John, floored by his brother's logic once more, and still finding himself inexplicably drawn to the cuteness of the robin family, followed him into the depths of the next bush.

Josh was busy lifting the loose undergrowth from the covered trap door. They had been concentrating so much on the underside of the door last time they encountered it that they had paid less attention to this side. Now they could see that it was completely covered in old moss which, under a thick bush in the most overgrown corner of the churchyard, went to explain why it had lain undiscovered for so long.

Josh tugged at the embedded metal ring and confirmed that it still moved relatively easily.

"Right", he said. "The plan, as you know, is to catch them in the act. We're presuming they're coming by sea, perhaps being dropped off by the *ghost ship* before it sails a bit further around the coast, perhaps just strolling along the beach. In any case, I think it's safest for us to use this end to go down and capture them in the middle when they're distracted by sheep. We'll need the nets, the torch, and go in wetsuits in case we need to go to the other end of the tunnel. Any questions?"

John thought it sounded a good plan but was secretly terrified and hoping the crooks would not show. "Err, what happens if we catch them?" he asked, somewhat sheepishly.

"We raise the alarm," said Josh. They discussed a few other details, but John did not like to query too much. Josh seemed to have it all worked out in his head.

They covered up the trapdoor again, crawled out from under the bush and returned to the cottage to help their dad. His opening question was, "How were the robins? Did you see them?" and John responded with such genuine enthusiasm it made Josh smile.

Eventually all the jobs seemed to be finished, packing was started, and John and Josh headed off to bed slightly earlier than normal, in the hope of getting a bit of rest before their night-time adventure and the time Josh had calculated they needed to leave, in conjunction with his new favourite book, the tide table booklet. They listened carefully to their dad's every move, worried that he wouldn't go to bed in time to allow them to make their escape. He seemed to be constantly going around the house, wiping things down, tidying up, packing things away. He clearly wanted the friends employing him to think he had done a good job, and that they were getting value for money and not just doing him a favour by giving him work.

Josh had to admit the house did look infinitely better than when he had first arrived, with a fresh coat of paint throughout, new fixtures and fittings and new tiles both in the bathroom and the kitchen, as well as the garden having had a spruce up.

There would be no chance of them getting out until Dad was asleep, because there was no separate hallway and they would have to try to sneak past him.

Eventually they heard him in the bathroom and then the tell-tale click of his bedroom door. Then they waited a good extra twenty minutes till they were sure he was asleep, hearing the sound of his snoring through the thin wall separating their rooms. They were already in their wetsuits, having put them on under their pyjamas as a precaution in case their dad checked in on them. He never did, but they were being extra cautious. If ever there was a night for their dad to start, it would have been tonight!

They decided to go out in their pyjamas, just in case their dad caught them on the way out. It would be far easier to make up an excuse for late night wandering in pyjamas than wetsuits, even if he noticed they were carrying bags full of fishing nets, ropes and a torch!

They crept along the landing, and down the stairs, picking up the key from the dresser and sneaking out of the front door, closing it as quietly as they could behind them. They had decided against shoes as getting in the way in the muddy tunnel, which had the added advantage of making their footsteps quieter. They crossed the road and hid themselves in the dark shadowy lychgate of the churchyard, where they took their pyjamas off to reveal their wetsuits, and stuffed them into John's waterproof bag which they hid in the shadowy corner of the gate. Josh added the house key.

"It's the safest place for it", he said. "Hopefully we won't get split up, but if we do, whoever gets back first can get back in the house if needed."

They silently padded through the churchyard to the overgrown corner and through the undergrowth to the bush hiding the trapdoor entrance. John found himself involuntarily glancing at the adjoining bush and thinking of the robins. He might well have imagined it, but he thought he heard one whistle a merry tune.

Under the bush they quickly pulled open the trapdoor and laid it flat open. Josh pulled out his torch and a short length of rope from his remaining bag, tied one end to the thick stem of the bush, and threw the other down the hole. "We may as well leave it open," he said, "I don't think anyone will notice at night, and this rope should help us climb back up without having to resort to piggy backs!" He checked his watch "We'd better be getting into positions. By my calculations they might be here soon."

He slipped carefully down the short drop into the tunnel, using the rope to aid him, quickly followed by John, telling himself he wanted to stay close to his little brother to make sure he was ok, but also partly not wanting to be left behind in the dark churchyard by himself.

They carefully made their way along the tunnel, hardly daring to talk, barely daring to breathe. It seemed darker than it was last time they were in the tunnel, but they knew this must just be an illusion – as before they were following a circle of torchlight ahead of them along the muddy floor of the tunnel.

In a few minutes, they came upon the pile of barrels and knew they were coming to the hole in the roof. They had agreed, in their whispered planning, that the best place to lay in wait to catch a thief, where they would be at the most advantage, was just outside the hole. They figured he must come out to catch a sheep and, if they could catch him as he emerged from the hole, they would have the element of surprise on their side. After first switching off the torch they listened carefully for any noise in the tunnel but since there was none, they climbed up the rope as quickly and quietly as they could, taking the largest of the fishing nets and hiding by the bush that partly covered the hole. They carefully positioned themselves so that anyone emerging from the hole would have their back to them, making it easy, they hoped, to throw the net over the top of them and restrain them, relying on the element of surprise.

Then they sat down to wait. And wait. And wait.

At first John was a bit scared, and Josh too. The first bleat they heard from a sleepy sheep made them jump, but every bleat thereafter made them jump slightly less, till in time they had been there so long they scarcely noticed the mutterings of the dozing sheep.

They did notice the cold coming through the damp grass, making them shiver in their wetsuits, and the cramp in their aching legs as they crouched in readiness, poised to throw the net over anyone emerging from the tunnel.

John found himself growing more and more sceptical - why had he so readily believed his brother's theory and gone along with his plans. Clearly, no one was coming, and they were just freezing in the process.

Josh, in turn, was having his own doubts, starting to fear he might have miscalculated, but he had been so sure…

Eventually, John was about to suggest that they gave up and went back to the cottage and to his longed-for bed. He thought he might fall asleep where he crouched if they stayed there much longer.

And that was when it happened.

As John had half-turned towards Josh to whisper the suggestion of giving up, he caught a glimpse of movement out of the corner of his eye. At the same time Josh nudged him, their agreed signal, and they turned and threw the net with full force over the dark shape rising from underground, finding new strength in their sore legs.

The shape gave a yelp of surprise, trapped lying flat on their front on the ground, having just pulled himself up the last of the rope and being unsure what was attacking him. Seizing their chance, Josh and John leaped on top to pin him down, and somehow managed to prise his arms out from between the gaps in the net and tie his wrists together behind his back, with another piece of rope Josh produced from his bag, managing to secure both the man and the net around him so he couldn't move.

Josh secured the loose end of the rope to the thick stem of the bush, just to make sure.

Josh and John had barely spoken a word to each other during this extraordinary process, they had planned so precisely that they knew exactly what they were doing. As a result, the surprised criminal was not entirely sure what had captured him, human or otherwise. It seemed like a giant sprawly rope monster had floored him and pinned him to the ground. To be fair, he'd probably been knocked breathless by the force of both boys landing on his back too. So he was both startled and dazed when Josh leaned close to his ear and whispered, "Don't worry, I'll be back," scarcely able to keep a note of triumph out of his voice, and then both boys promptly disappeared back down the hole by the flailing robber's feet, and he was left wondering if he'd imagined them and just accidentally knocked himself on the head or something else which might explain his inability to move.

In the tunnel, Josh switched on his torch again and grinned at John, who could not resist grinning back. It felt good to be moving again after being inactive for so long. They looked around the tunnel, there was a barrel prepared with its lid off, ready for its cargo. If they'd been more attentive, they might have heard the sounds of the barrel being moved in the tunnel below. Still, they had another job to do now and started to carefully make their way towards the sea end of the tunnel. The water seemed to be deeper than they remembered at this stage of the tunnel last time, and quickly got deeper still. The boys put on their snorkels and masks, prepared and ready to swim when necessary.

There seemed to be a bit of a current in the water, with it ebbing and flowing back up the tunnel. Josh surmised this might be because the sea end of the tunnel was open, so the water in the tunnel was flowing in with the tide. John and Josh carried a net each, and it was hard to keep going when the water was weighing them down. Eventually, before they got out of their depth, Josh took both ropes and put them in the carrier bag, hoping any remaining air in the carrier bag would help them to float. Nearer the exit they could take them out again, ready for whatever lay in wait for them at the other end of the tunnel.

All too quickly they reached the stage of having to swim, but still managed to keep their heads above water. Eventually from the depth of the water and the force of the current Josh could sense that they were nearing the end of the tunnel. He took one of the nets out of the bag, switched off his torch, put that in the bag and handed it behind him to John.

"I'll go first" he whispered, "If I don't capture him, you can come behind and help."

John's tummy felt like a flutter of butterflies. He thought maybe he should be going first, but was relieved there was no arguing with Josh when he was this set in his mind to do something. At the same time he was feeling nervously responsible for backing Josh up in any way he could. He just took the bag and whispered, "Good luck," as he watched Josh dive through the last stretch of deep water that was nearly up to the roof of the tunnel, and prayed the element of surprise would work in their favour this time too.

Josh plunged on through the water, hoping the air at the top of the snorkel would not run out. He tried not to get disorientated, but it was hard to see through his mask with the water rushing quickly past. He sensed, rather than saw, the trapdoor approaching. He tried to hold the net out in front of him whilst swimming forward, hoping he could time his capture correctly.

The net was heavy in the water as he kicked forwards with his feet and in an instant emerged spluttering into the cold dark air, trying to get his bearings. Before him was a man dressed in dark clothes. He was sure it was the same one he had glimpsed before on the rock that night. He tried to thrust the net out in front of him and around the man, but the man, despite being taken by surprise, grabbed hold of the net and swivelled round, taking both net and Josh who was holding on to it firmly and pivoting them both into the dark waters of the sea.

Josh had a fleeting moment of panic, imagining both himself and the unknown crook drowning in the murky depths, drifting out to sea and never being seen again.

It was only a fleeting moment, however, as John catapulted out of the water and rapidly realising the situation, managed to throw his net over the flailing thief, who was too concerned about keeping afloat to put up much of a fight. He, like his partner in crime was now trapped.

In a smooth move John managed to grab the other end of the net that Josh was still gripping firmly, pulling both sheep stealer and sibling to shore. Thankfully, it was only a matter of metres, and John could tell easily which direction to go in, heading from the glimmer of the moonlight on the waves to the blackness of the beach. John was a much stronger swimmer than his brother, but even he still felt exhausted with the effort of dragging them both to land.

Josh found his feet touching the bottom and managed to start paddling, able to steady himself enough to help John with the trussed thief, escorting him, one on each side, up the beach. Thankfully, the man didn't seem much taller than John, and in his bound state the two could manage him relatively easily. He seemed too resigned to put up much resistance.

"Erm, where shall we head to first?" asked John, trying not to sound too doubtful in front of their captive, but not really having a clue what to do next. He was thankful when his brother exuded the new confidence he had seen in him over the past week.

"Don't worry, I know exactly where we're going."

Inwardly, Josh silently gulped down his fear. There was no doubt in his mind where they needed to go, but this knowledge did not calm his fears in the least.

He could just make out the gap in the cliffs ahead where he had glimpsed those mysterious picnic benches on his very first trip to this beach, which now seemed so long ago. He knew it would be too far to escort their mostly silent prisoner back to the cottage and there was only one occupied building nearby that he knew of and that was where they had to go. The only slight flaw was that he'd never been there before and didn't know exactly where it was, not to mention the fact that he was significantly scared of its occupant.

As he got through the gap in the shallow cliffs and past the picnic benches, he was relieved to see a small light shining from a window not too far away, and they headed straight for it, pushing their captive ahead of them.

Chapter Nineteen

EXPLAIN

SLOWLY an outline of a building emerged from the gloom and John worked out where Josh was taking them. Standing outside the farmhouse door, Josh took a deep breath, took one hand off their confused criminal, and knocked loudly, praying for a warmer welcome than he feared they'd get. He could hear his heart thudding loudly in his chest as they waited in silence for an answer.

A gruff voice came from inside, "Who is it? What do you want?"

Josh decided politeness was the best policy: "I'm so sorry to disturb you, sir, especially at this time of night, but we've caught the people who were stealing your sheep."

He heard bolts being drawn back rapidly and the shocked look on the face of the well-built farmer turned to pure astonishment at the sight of the two boys escorting the net-bound criminal between them. He shone a powerful flashlight on each of them in turn, then back at Josh again as a flutter of recognition appeared in his eyes. "But you're…you're just boys…how did you manage….? Do I know you? I've seen your face before."

"Yes, sir, I met you at church, sir," continued Josh nervously, hoping this was not too inaccurate a summary of his remembrance of cowering in fear and trying to avoid the intimidating farmer after the Sunday service. "Could I suggest you phone the police please, sir. There's another one we've trapped in the middle of the field as well?"

The farmer, no longer scary, seemed lost for words, in his complete amazement, but quickly made an effort to pull himself together and take control of the situation and work out what to do. "Right then, I'll do that in a minute but first let's deal with this one." He picked up a key from a small table next to the door and then stepped out towards them, "If you wouldn't mind bringing your, ahem, *friend* there just this way a bit, I think he'll be safe in here for a bit; allow me."

The farmer unlocked a small outbuilding adjoining the farmhouse with one hand, and with the other took the arm of their prisoner from them and propelled him inside, locking the door behind him. Josh and John felt relieved to be free of their burden, and glad someone else was taking charge.

"Now, did you say there was another one?" he asked. "Should we see to him first, or will he keep while I quickly phone the police?"

"I think we secured him well," ventured John, "He'll keep for an extra couple of minutes."

"Oh, ok then," said the farmer, "Give me a minute and I'll give them a ring. I guess you'd better come in." Leaving them hesitating on the threshold, he disappeared inside. Conscious they were still in slightly dripping wetsuits, Josh and John heard a muffled, one-sided conversation coming from within. The farmer sounded insistent and assertive and, true to his word, reappeared precisely a minute later. "The police are on their way. So where did you leave this other one then? And at some point you'd better explain how you caught them? And maybe how they took my sheep! But I guess that can wait till the police arrive…" The farmer seemed to have become quite talkative. "They took a bit of persuading though. I told them I had a sheep rustler locked up in my outbuilding. They seemed a bit surprised when they asked how I caught him and I said two boys turned up on my doorstep in the middle of the night with him wrapped up in a fishing net!"

Whilst the farmer was talking, Josh was leading them forwards, slightly hesitantly as he'd never been to the section of the farmer's field they'd left the crook in overground before, only through the tunnel! Thankfully he'd carefully memorised its position the first time he had discovered the hole in the tunnel, in order to be able to find it again. Also, as they had now been outside for several hours, his eyes were well-adjusted to darkness and he could more or less work out surrounding landmarks in the shimmering moonlight. Soon they heard the sound of grunting, where the first trussed criminal was trying fruitlessly and half-heartedly to escape from his rope and net bindings. They headed straight for him, aided by the noise he was making.

The farmer seemed impressed at this other captive, and Josh and John were secretly relieved that he was still where they had left him. Josh headed for where he had attached the rope to the bush and fumbled with the knot.

"Here, let me," said the farmer, coming up behind him. Josh stepped aside and the farmer pulled a penknife out of his pocket and, with a deft move, sliced through the rope, took the end, and started leading the prisoner back to the farmhouse with a "Come on then, let's be having you!"

They had just locked him in a second outbuilding when the police arrived. With the relief that their two captives were safely stowed away and ready for removal by the police, the adrenalin that had kept them going started to fade and Josh gave an involuntary shiver. This caught the farmer's attention, and he seemed to notice for the first time their bare feet and dripping hair. "Right, come on in you two, you must be freezing. Let's get you inside and warmed up so you can tell these two officers how you managed to catch the thieves in the act."

He escorted them all inside, into a large living room, comfortably if sparsely furnished, disappeared for a minute, and came back with two large rough towels and handed one each to the boys, who had been hesitating to sit down in the plump, old-fashioned armchairs, reluctant to drip on the furniture. "Wrap yourselves in these and take a seat."

There were some glowing embers in the fireplace and, after a quick rake through them, the farmer added some logs and twigs and left the room again. The fire burst back into life, warming flames leaping up towards the chimney. Josh and John were grateful for the heat it threw out, as warmth seeped back into their feet and fingers, which in all the excitement they had not realised had become nearly numb.

The two police officers, a man and a woman, remained silent, clearly following the farmer's lead in giving them a chance to warm up first, and not wanting to start asking questions in his absence.

The farmer soon returned with a tray bearing five mugs, three of tea for himself and the police officers, and two of steaming hot chocolate which he placed before the grateful boys, grinning, "Hopefully these should warm you up!"

Josh started to wonder how he could ever have found him scary.

With hot chocolate mug in hand, and John encouraging Josh to take the lead in the telling, Josh related his tale as succinctly as possible to the surprised but admiring farmer and police. He told how from his first suspicions he had slowly uncovered clues which had let ultimately to his unravelling of the mystery and his daring plan to catch the criminals in the act.

He deliberately glossed over his early suspicions that the farmer might be involved in smuggling, elicited astonished looks when he mentioned the discovery of the tunnel and their exploration of it, and made them even more amazed when he explained the barrel system and how the thieves had got the sheep off the farm without anyone noticing.

"So that's how the blighters did it without being picked up on my CCTV!" exclaimed the farmer and Josh caught a glimpse of his old rage.

He ended his tale with a statement of his belief that there was a boat further down the coast, possibly disguised as a ghost ship, to which the barrels lead, and an urgent plea to the police to send some of their colleagues to intercept it and catch any more crooks who might be onboard. The female police officer immediately radioed this information through to the station and assured the boys it would be dealt with straightaway.

Josh and John were relieved to have matters taken out of their hands and things wrapped up as much as they could be, but alarmed by the male officer's last question, "So, do you think we should go let your dad know what you two have been up to, then?"

"Please," said John. "Could we possibly leave that till the morning. He'll only worry and we're all safe now?"

"And he's been working hard, he's really tired," added Josh, in a desperate plea to postpone the inevitable.

"Oh, ok," conceded the female officer," I suppose we could leave it till then. If we pop round at nine a.m. to let him know and give you an update, would that be suitable? I think you've given us the address," she added, checking her notebook.

"Yes, thanks," said Josh and John in unison, grateful for this brief reprieve, worried what their dad would say when he found out about their exploits.

"Right then," said the farmer, asserting himself once more and addressing the officers. "If you wouldn't mind removing those two criminals from my outhouses, I'll make sure the boys get safely back to their cottage."

"Thanks," said the first officer, "if you wouldn't mind unlocking them for us, we'll take them away." Then he turned to the boys "And well done lads! You've been very brave and clever in solving this crime, if a little foolhardy in acting alone. Next time you solve a mystery, let us know and we can apprehend the suspects for you."

With that parting shot the police followed the farmer out of the room and Josh muttered to John, "I bet they'd never have believed us though!"

After a short while they heard the police car drive away and the farmer came back, and they found themselves reluctant at the prospect of leaving the warm room and going out into the cold darkness again. "I bet you two are dead on your feet, aren't you? It's not far, but I'll take you back in my Land Rover."

A short trip later and he deposited them outside the church, a few doors down from the cottage.

"Don't want to wake dad just yet," said Josh. "And besides, we need to collect something."

The farmer watched as they leapt out and pulled the bag out of the shadows of the church's lychgate. As they passed him again, to cross back over the road to the cottage, he wound the window down and called out to them in a loud whisper, "Thanks boys, for all you've done. I really appreciate it. It means a lot."

Both boys got the distinct impression that this brief statement was an expression of unusual sincerity and openness for the usually gruff farmer, and they gave him a cheery but silent wave as they crossed the road.

Josh fished in the bag for the key, and they let themselves as silently as they could back into the cottage. They wrestled their way as noiselessly as they could out of their wetsuits and clambered wearily back into their pyjamas and into bed. It had been an exciting night, but they were ready for sleep now.

They abandoned their wetsuits in the middle of the floor. There was no point hiding them any longer. In the morning, for better or worse, their dad would know the truth.

Chapter Twenty

CHAMPAGNE

AT the church fete the next day, the brothers were feeling a mix of emotions: elation, that they had solved the mystery and caught the criminals, exhaustion from their tiring night, and relief that their dad hadn't taken it too badly.

When they woke up that morning the police officers were already there, talking in hushed tones to their dad, so as not to wake them. They had listened carefully and caught the odd word, though, to work out if it was safe to go downstairs or not. When they heard the words *heroes* and *astoundingly brave* they had decided it was as good a time as any to make an entrance.

Their dad had had a mix of emotions too, from confusion and fear at discovering the police at the door, astonishment at their account of the boys' achievements, and belated worry as to what might have happened to them. Ultimately, he'd settled on being proud of them, after a brief stern warning to tell him first next time they planned on catching crooks. There was no point worrying after the event.

As well as breaking the news to their dad, the police had brought further news that a third criminal had been arrested on a suspicious boat, which had also been seized after significant amounts of sheep wool were found in its hold, giving a clue as to its recent cargo. The two men the boys had caught had confessed to the sheep thefts. Having practically been caught in the act, they did not have much choice or chance of evading justice.

Walking around the fete, on the field by the playground, both the boys and their dad were trying to chill, enjoying having a go at throwing hard balls at the coconut shy, browsing through assorted treasures on the bric-a-brac stall, and all three of them failing hysterically at splatting the rat, a game involving hitting a beanbag against a board, after it had been launched through a tube and before it hit the floor, or not as the case proved!

"I think maybe you two need to get more sleep," smiled their dad knowingly. "It might speed up your reactions a bit!"

"I'll have you know we were spot on with our criminal catching reactions last night!" joked Josh.

"Yes, apart from the one I had to fish out of the sea for you," teased John, omitting, as their dad was there, that he had effectively had to fish Josh out of the sea too.

Josh resisted retaliating as he saw Owain, the vicar, making a beeline for them.

"Ah, I'm so glad you could make it, and I'm glad to have caught you before you head back home. I'll catch up with you shortly, I just need to make an announcement. Don't go anywhere!" And, almost inexplicably after the initial beeline he had made, the vicar did a U-turn and headed for the microphone at the front of the field, proceeding to tap on it, both to test it and get people's attention.

"Hello, hello, can you all hear me? Good! I'd just like your attention for a few moments please. Firstly, I'd like to thank you all for coming today and spending what you can. I'd like to remind you that every penny spent today goes towards helping the unemployed and poor in this area. We really appreciate your help. But, actually, what I'd really like to express is some appreciation for a great contribution to this community, made by some people who have only visited us recently, but have truly influenced this area for the better."

Josh felt his mind starting to drift slightly, helped by his exhaustion, as it sometimes did during the vicar's sermons. He was jolted to attention though by the vicar's next words. "Josh and John, can you come forwards please?"

Equally shocked, John pulled himself together first, grabbed Josh's arm so he didn't have to go forwards alone, and propelled him towards the vicar. Owain extended a welcoming arm towards them, a smile on his face. "Josh and John, sorry if I've taken you by surprise! Well, actually, that was kind of the idea, but anyway…Let me introduce you to everyone. I'm not sure they've all met you yet, I've scarcely met John myself!" He turned to the amassed crowd and pointed to each boy in turn, "This is Josh, he's only been staying here a few weeks. And this is John, who has been here less than a week. And yet these two have managed, through amazing deduction skills and an astonishing act of bravery to do a great service to this community. Last night these two brave lads caught the sheep rustlers that have been plaguing our area. They captured them, raised the alarm and the crafty criminals are now in the custody of the police."

Ooos and *Ahhs* of amazement and appreciation went up from the crowd.

The vicar waited for them to subside before carrying on. "The boys are due to return home with their dad today, but before they do, we'd like to present them with a special award. For this I would like to invite Jac to come and help."

The farmer emerged from the crowd where, somehow, the boys had failed to notice him. He was carrying two framed certificates and had a slightly sheepish grin on his face as he came to the microphone, clearly unused to public speaking, and appearing slightly lost for words.

"Josh and John…John and Josh… I just want to say thank you. Thank you for coming to visit our little village. Thank you for taking the time to solve our mystery that has perplexed me and the police for a long time. Thank you for having the outrageous daring to catch those criminals in the act and turn up on my doorstep with them in the middle of the night last night. In recognition of your bravery and your help for the community of Aberfawr, I'd like to present each of you with these bravery awards." He handed each of them a framed certificate. "We really appreciate all you've done."

"Hear, hear!" shouted the vicar, and the crowd erupted into applause, before, eventually, at a signal from Owain, dispersing back into their own conversations, leaving the boys stunned and looking at each other between the vicar and the farmer.

"Well done!" grinned the vicar, patting each of them on the back, "Do come back and visit us sometime, anytime. We'd be delighted to see you again."

"Actually, about that," said Jac the farmer, still slightly awkward in his manner. "I don't know if you know, but I have a holiday cottage and a couple of camping pods on my farm."

Ah, thought Josh, this was the obvious deduction from the first glimpse of those picnic benches that he'd missed. He obviously wasn't that good at solving mysteries after all.

But the farmer was continuing "I'd be more than happy for you to come and stay in whichever of them you like, whenever you like, for free. It's the least I can do for all you've done for me. Have you heard the police are optimistic they might be able to get some of my stolen sheep back, now they've worked out where they were being taken? You've saved me a lot of money and stress."

Josh was too shocked to talk, but hoped his grin showed appreciation and thankfully John managed to get out, "Thank you, that's very kind."

"And I wanted to say thank you too," said the vicar, joining in, and also lowering his tone, "I hear you've discovered the church's long-lost tunnel. I didn't want to make it public yet till we can make sure it's safe; we don't want people exploring and injuring themselves, but I'm so excited about it! I'm sure we can get a grant to help restore it and open the less watery part up to the public. I think it could be just what we need to draw more tourists into the village. We can take donations for admission and the money raised will be really helpful in helping us continue our work with the unemployed and poor in the parish. Sadly, there are a lot of impoverished people in the area." He glanced up and noticed that Jac had been engaged in conversation by an acquaintance a short distance away, enabling him to speak frankly. "Lots of the farmers in particular have suffered really hard times, and this sheep rustling didn't help."

Owain looked up to discover a flustered young man coming towards them, with a camera round his neck. John and Josh followed the vicar's gaze as the man spoke. "Sorry I'm late, Owain, I got stuck in traffic. Have I missed it?"

"I'm afraid you have," laughed the vicar, "But nothing we can't recreate for you. Come back over here a sec please Jac!" and he beckoned the farmer back. "This is Thomas from the Herald," he said by way of explanation to all of them, "You don't mind posing for him, do you?" And, without waiting for a reply, he lined up John and Josh between himself and Jac, reclaimed the framed certificates from the stunned boys, handed one to Jac so he could pose presenting it to John, whilst he himself held out the other one towards Josh, both angled carefully towards the tardy journalist. "That ok for you, Thomas?"

"Perfect," said the grateful reporter, relieved he hadn't missed the story entirely, and clicking the button on his camera with a blinding flash. He took a few more shots, then checked his camera. "That should do, thanks," he said and got his notebook out. "If I could just ask a few questions of the brave pair?"

But after a couple of hastily thought up answers to how they were feeling, the vicar escorted them away back towards their waving dad. I can give you the rest of the details Thomas. These two have a train to catch. Thanks again boys, well done, and I'll post you your picture from the paper!"

"What just happened?" said John to Josh as they stumbled towards their dad who was anxiously looking at his watch, concerned about them missing the bus to the station. But they were interrupted again by the vicar's wife, anxious to say a quick goodbye, and thrusting a polythene bag on them tied up with an elaborate ribbon, which turned out to contain half a dozen chunky chocolate chip cookies.

"Farewell, Josh and John, and Darren too. Hope you have a good journey. I just got these from the cake stall and thought they'd help keep you going till you get back home." She then turned to Darren and handed him a similarly-wrapped bottle out of her bag. "And I just won this on the bottle tombola - champagne! I thought you could toast your clever sons with your wife when you get back home."

They all chipped in their thanks, but then Darren said, "Sorry to hurry you boys, but our bus to the station goes soon and we need to collect all our things out of the cottage and get to the bus stop in super quick time!"

"Don't worry!" boomed a deep voice from behind John and Josh making them jump.

They turned to see Jac approaching them hurriedly. "I'll take you to the station. It's the least I can do, delaying you by giving you bravery awards!" He winked at the boys. "Just let me get my Land Rover. I'll be outside your cottage in five minutes."

"Well, if you're sure," muttered Darren. "We'd be very grateful." But, clearly, they didn't need to agree, as Jac was already striding off into the distance to fulfil his promise. Instead Darren turned to his sons, both awkwardly clutching their certificates, "I'm proud of you boys. You know that don't you? Now let's get moving! We need to get you back home. It'll soon be time for school to start again."

And they hurried back to the cottage to grab their stuff, ready for the trip to the station with Jac and the long train journey home. The summer had turned out to be much more eventful than they could ever have expected.

THE END

ANOTHER BOOK YOU MIGHT ENJOY

JOFFIE'S MARK by MARK PECKETT

Joffie is fifteen, an orphan and thief, surviving in Victorian Beormingham on her wits and her peculiar talent - the ability to find secret doorways between worlds. Trouble looms when she steals a mysterious cane from a toff and her ensuing adventures place her in mortal danger. And unless she can free a long-forgotten god she and her friends are doomed...

(APS Books 2022)

Printed in Great Britain
by Amazon